BOOKS BY EILEEN SAINT LAUREN

Goodlife, Mississippi   A Novel

Southern Light, Oxford, Mississippi

Southern Light, Oxford, Mississippi

Eileen Saint Lauren

EILEEN SAINT LAUREN BOOKS
CHAPEL HILL, NC (USA)

EILEEN SAINT LAUREN BOOKS
CHAPEL HILL, NC (USA)

SOUTHERN LIGHT, OXFORD, MISSISSIPPI
Copyright © 2023 by Eileen Saint Lauren

ISBN 979-8-9861963-5-0
1. Southern Gothic—Fiction 2. Historical Fiction 3. Literature of the American South—Segregation, Mississippi. Title

Book Design by Arash Jahani

Unless otherwise noted, the Bible version used in this publication is THE KING JAMES VERSION, Copyright © 1972 Thomas Nelson, Inc., Publishers.

This is a work of fiction. Names, characters, businesses, places, events, and incidents are either the products of the author's imagination or used in a fictitious manner. Any resemblance to actual persons, living or dead, or actual events is purely coincidental.

Dedicated to everyone—dead or alive—that has ever wanted to be a writer. And I dedicate this book to all who were harmed in unspeakable ways by someone they trusted.

Contents

Southern Light, Oxford, Mississippi

Preface

After graduating from Jones College in Ellisville, Mississippi, I entered the University of Nebraska at Lincoln as an older student. One of my professors was a William Faulkner scholar *and* Mississippi-born like me. Drunk and sober, he shared many stories of his experiences—some real, some no doubt imagined—of Faulkner having been a personal friend and once a drinking partner. He told me that he was present when Faulkner *finally* delivered his acceptance speech for the Nobel Prize in Literature in Stockholm, Sweden. I was given the professor's gifts of goodwill and enthusiasm resulting in his filling my mind with everything Faulkner. I so closely identified with Faulkner's discursiveness, obscurities, and satire that I was inspired to write a screenplay with William Faulkner as one of the characters for my then screenwriting class, a screenplay that many years later I turned into the novel *Southern Light, Oxford, Mississippi*.

Southern Light, Oxford, Mississippi is my humble effort to create a book that the reader can get an essence of what I came to believe were William Faulkner's thoughts about writing, the Deep South, Hollywood, God, and more. I hope that you enjoy reading it as much as I enjoyed writing it. My best wishes to you, Eileen Saint Lauren

SOUTHERN LIGHT

Chapter 1

Mississippi winters in Oxford have always been bone-cold and filled with hidden turbulences that stir the soul, leaving folks not knowing what to expect from one hour to the next, from one year to the next, and one minute the sun's penetrating rays will burst through, making a body feel like it's hell's center; then as suddenly, the dark clouds move in and bring rain to cleanse the souls—dead or alive and that's when a body can step out of hell's center into pastures new, and the snow—when it comes, it has been known to stir the dead; folklore itself will argue that God is altering the elements from a secret place, causing a rift in the azure dome; all of this moves me to silent laughter because I strongly believe by the time you read this book, and as the winds howl on around the corners of Fable Court, I'll be dead and in the ground, though I don't expect anyone to understand *why* I felt I had to do what I had to do to survive the pain that comes with love because no one has ever understood me any more than they've understood what's inside the human heart save for God—yes, God; I believe that God understands me *and* all the other writers out there as we channel onto paper whoever or whatever enters our minds, then imaginations, so that we can finally feel some relief when we put our pencils and paper down at night … and alas, it was one lonely King Winter in 1879, before the death of his beloved wife, Camille, when Claude Monet had already begun to paint *Lavacourt: Sunshine and Snow* to take his mind off his problems, I write, in part, to take my mind off mine—now that's *my* truth; and as legend goes here in Mississippi, in the winter, when the Southern light meets the winter's snow, all hell can break loose and the emotional turbulence is enough to wake the dead or at least see that they are buried properly; this Oxford winter will be no different.

—Dec. 25, 1940, Fable Court

INVITATION

Chapter 2

December 7, 1960

Winter 3:30 a.m. — cold

Dearest Mary and Joe,

Greetings! I hope this piece of correspondence finds you both well and happy. I am quite well except for my eyes. They pain me so sometimes that I feel like someone is jabbing at my mind as well as my eyes with an ice pick. I am afraid that there is something other than cataracts in them that is sending pain to my brain, making it laugh at me like a cloud of darkness in the

*midst of a bad storm. Sometimes, I find that I am just not myself,
and I find that I shed new tears when I look into the mirror.
Doctor Moss, my doctor from New Orleans, said that my ice pick
headaches will soon pass, but I doubt his words.*

*Never mind me and my murmurs on paper because the reason
that I am writing to you two is that I want to give you a little
wedding present to make up for not being able to attend your
wedding day last month. My beloved Edward left me more than
enough as far as earthly security goes, so I feel that I must share
some of my good fortune with as many folks as I can. Therefore,
I am offering you some free land as a belated wedding gift. It's
mighty fine land, and it is loaded with the rich, natural growing
powers that can only be found amid the Southern light in
Mississippi.*

*For many years, I have shunned most folks in Oxford because
even though they speak, their words are filled with the emptiness
of an old, worn sugar spoon. They cause me more grief asking
about Edward and all. For now, I want some of my own flesh and
blood kin near me before I go on Home to be with my dear
Edward. I may not die poor or neglected, but I want some of my*

blood kin near me when I go — I don't want to die alone. I will be 88 December 25, 1960. If you two will come and stay for my birthday, I will be satisfied. I won't make you take the free land if you do not agree as man and wife that you want to live in Oxford. Come prepared to stay for Christmas and my birthday if you don't mind because I feel like it won't be long before the Lord calls my name.

Tell Joe if he's interested at all in meeting my neighbor, Mr. William Faulkner, I will invite him over for a bit of refreshments and biscuits, Scotch whiskey for Mr. Faulkner, on Christmas Eve. And, perhaps, we can all decorate a tree together in the parlor. Mr. Faulkner is often quite free to leave his home, Rowan Oak, these days though he has been ill for many months now. I'll include his wife, Estelle, in the invitation too. In case you forgot, I live alone at Number 33 Fable Court, right down the road from where the bend in Garfield Road takes its steep turn at the end of Beacon Street — half a mile or so from Rowan Oak. In fact, sometimes I see William walking with his Jack Russell Terriers down the well-worn paths that the land workers make visible after each new harvest. He'll tip his hat at me and smile. He is as white-headed as he can be. I would say that he is just as lonely as I am.

Indeed, I am overjoyed that you may be coming all the way from Meridian to see me! If you don't mind, would you bring me a glass of "mint-flavored" snuff made by the R. J. Reynolds Tobacco Company? I haven't had any of the mint-flavor in years it seems—since my New England days with Poppa. I would be much obliged if you all will. You can find a little store in Increase about twelve miles right outside of Meridian called Causeyville General Store. Tell Joe to take MS 19 South and then follow the signs on the Meridian-Causeyville Road. The "mint-flavored" snuff can serve as my birthday surprise.
Ha-ha!

I will close for now as it is hot and humid enough to grow an indoor vegetable garden in this Reading Room. In fact, the old pianoforte that Edward gave me from New England for our first wedding anniversary seems to be sweating like early morning dew on my hibiscuses. The light is out for some reason. I will have to hang a new oatmeal lid string up in here until someone comes by to repair it for me. I have one servant nowadays—Mordecai

Malachi. He has looked after me, Layne, and Julius Caesar since Edward disappeared. If not for Mordecai, I don't know what I would do! I will be anxiously awaiting your arrival. One more request from this old woman: Please bring the spirit of Christmas with you to Fable Court. Often it feels like death lingers amid its walls...

My heart will always be open for you,

Aunt Eleanor Franklin

Number 33 Beacon Street Fable Court

Oxford, Mississippi 38655

662-234-7734

P.S. Don't forget my glass of "mint-flavored" snuff!

FABLE COURT, DECEMBER 7, 1960, OXFORD, MISSISSIPPI—4 A.M.

Chapter 3

AN AGED GERMAN MAN, still strong of stature and alert but seeming to belong to another place and to this world at the same time, Mordecai Malachi, is arranging colorful mosaic tiles on the wall of a long sharply arched hallway to form images that will one day tell their stories. He breaks from his work to reach for a memory book resting on a stool in an alcove in the wall. With a quill, he begins to copy sentences from William Shakespeare's *King Lear* on a blank page. He reads aloud, "This cold night will turn us all to fools and madmen. Child Layne to the dark tower came, His word was still—Fie, foh, and fum, I smell the blood of a dead Man."

From behind the wall a voice asks, "Mordecai, that you? Let me out. Nature has brought in a mouse. I can feel it with my hands. Ouch!" There is a gasp for air then comes, "No, wait—it's a sparrow."

Mordecai takes notice. He does nothing other than cock his head towards another part of Fable Court where a frail little old white-headed lady, Eleanor Franklin, and a Persian cat are stirring to get dressed.

"Julius Caesar be patient. We'll eat when we get back," Eleanor tells the cat. She pats him on the head and then taps his nose three times with her pointer finger. "You hear?"

Julius Caesar looks up at Eleanor. He gives her an understanding meow.

She smiles at him. Her skeleton small and spare. Her voice dry and cold.

Julius Caesar is snow-white in color. He has one yellow eye and one blue eye with long gray whiskers that stick out from under a pink glass marble-like nose. Eleanor Franklin is dressing him in a navy-blue suede jacket with a white fur collar with the gold letters J C monogrammed along both sides. She puts on an old green Egyptian-like velvet shawl that ties in the front. She places a pair of dark spectacles into a patent leather purse. She shrugs her shoulders and squeals a little with excitement. She gives a fond look into an oval mirror at herself. The mirror has no frame.

Mordecai cocks his head to the left, detecting the voice of Eleanor and the stirring sounds of Julius Caesar. Upon finishing his last sentence, he reads it aloud, "Think free. Be patient." He peeps through two holes in the alcove before saying, "Still, you are a sight for the eyes." He turns to put his quill away. He walks toward the hallway door when the voice begins to cry out from behind the wall mosaic, "Mordecai, why must you stop writing so early? You all I got."

"The worst is not—So long as we can say 'This is the worst,'" Mordecai replies to the voice.

What he has seen is a small in stature, man-child sitting on the floor behind the wall mosaic in a room papered with forest green wallpaper dotted with silver lilies with brown and green stems threaded with gold. The boy is stroking an animal that appears to be a sparrow, although it could be a squirrel or a mouse. He is wearing a black leather patch over his right eye.

"Hey, boy!" he says, whistling instinctively to the small animal while stroking its head. He begins to rock like a scared child when he senses that Mordecai has stopped his writing, fearing that he has been left alone prompting, "Mordecai? YOU there? Mordecai?"

No answer.

When he realizes that he's been left alone with himself, he screams.

Mordecai walks into the other part of the house where Eleanor and Julius Caesar are leaving Fable Court. He grabs his overcoat and lingers close behind in the quiet darkness. Julius Caesar notices him, but not Eleanor. Both begin a brisk walk along Garfield Road. They pass an antebellum house with a sign posted out front that reads *Rowan Oak*. She sees a faint light burning in one of the rainbow-hued Depression glass windows. At once she believes that she's in Jefferson, Yoknapatawpha County, William Faulkner's imaginary town.

"Julius, do you suppose that the people of Jefferson are awake yet? I see a light burning in William's window. See it?" Eleanor asks her cat. He doesn't answer. He looks over at a window that is half-hidden beneath the shadows of an old oak tree. Eleanor sees the light flicker in the window. Her mind escapes her, taking her to the middle of a Monday in Jefferson, Mississippi, sometime around the turn of the century. She walks on and begins to imagine that Jefferson's streets are filled with people. Some streets are paved; some are not. Oaks, maples, locusts, and elms line the streets of the town. A laundry truck makes its Monday morning rounds, gathering bundles of soiled clothes from the White folks. She sees a schoolteacher with her students in tow, a storekeeper standing in front of his store sweeping the dirt, a prescription salesman with his suitcase of drugs walking briskly down the road, some ancient maidens, well-to-do lawyers, and various businessmen. Her thoughts take her on a higher flight causing her to hear them talking amongst themselves and occasionally speaking to her and Julius Caesar.

"Ladies, could I interest you in a bottle of *Godfrey's Cordial?* Buy one pint and get yourself a six-ounce bottle free!" cries a tonic salesman. He pauses to hold up a slim blue glass bottle before crying out to a group of ladies, "There is *Life* in this here bottle. Better than any vit-a-min you've ever tried. *Guar-ran-teed!*" He walks along his way.

The sun is spinning in Jefferson. The Mississippi humidity is so thick that you can cut it with a butcher knife. The tonic salesman reaches into his little leather black carrying case, pulls out a cardboard fan with Battle of Culloden on it, and fans himself.

A schoolteacher throws him a stern look. "Hurry along now children. Opium in a bottle. Iron liquor! I'm a mind to call the jailer to that *devil* liar. Children, hurry along now, I say." The children bustle along giving quick and shy glances at the noisy tonic salesman who stops to politely tip his hat at the lot of them. Their teacher points them in the direction of Euclid Street.

Eleanor smiles to herself. She walks along the road her mind now engulfed in Faulkner's imaginary town. She begins to talk with the spirits she sees in her mind. "Good morning. Hello. How you? Julius Caesar and I are on our way to see Edward. Why, thank you kindly. We will." She pauses and recognizes a lady. "No, Melicent, Layne isn't with us today." She gives the lady a reserved smile. "Of course, we'll tell him you said, hello. Won't we Julius?" She waves to the spirits in slow motion she sees approaching her and Julius Caesar. "Hello, Caddy and Jason. Dilsey, is that you?" She clutches her chest.

"Get the cure for Black Lung right here. *Godfrey's Cordial*—a miracle from the Lord God!" the tonic salesman cries out.

Eleanor becomes worried. When her mind moves her along with scenes from the past to the present, she begins to walk faster. "Oh my, come along, Julius. I don't want you to be exposed to *Black Lung*. Layne might catch it from you. You know how sensitive he is." She gasps for some air. "There's Jesus and Nancy. Oh my, what *is* Jesus doing? *What does he mean?* Oh, oh!" she says, seeing Jesus murder Nancy. She runs ahead. Julius Caesar follows close at her heels with his initials snaking down his back. Mordecai is still following but hanging back out of sight. After a short sprint, they arrive at the front gate of Saint Peter's Cemetery. Eleanor reaches into her purse, pulls out a long antique key with a flower motif at its head and unlocks the front gate. She and Julius Caesar walk into a floating fog. Mordecai ducks behind an oak tree.

Some of the headstones read—*Stringer, Thankful, Sheegog, Bailey, Sutpen, Charlie Davis, Lorena R-Cola Reynolds Davis, Claude and Claudine Davis—twins—born dead.* The twins' heart-shaped headstone bears the saying, *Out of the rock flows living water; this can be measured by mankind, but out of the heart flows the pure wine of our love for you our two now Angels. December 26, 1953, Love always, Momma and Poppa.*

Eleanor looks around Saint Peter's Cemetery.

Julius Caesar hisses.

"Hush up, Julius! You'll wake up the dead! No words, no words! Hush," Eleanor scolds her cat. They make their way to the back-right corner of the cemetery near a huge red Verona Italian marble mausoleum with a spiked gate of steel around it. She reaches into her purse for a small antique key that has a little honeybee at the base of its head. She uses it to unlock the gate. They stroll on inside to the Franklin mausoleum.

Mordecai doesn't follow. Instead, he walks towards a little deserted woodshed and changes into a caretaker's suit. He grabs a shovel from behind the shed's door. He unzips his suit, reaches down into his own front pants' pocket, pulls out a gold pocket watch, and gives it a long, silent stare before walking out into the floating fog. He stops and considers a plot of land before he begins digging a grave by the last light of the moon. Then as dry dirt, mixed with fresh, red-orange Mississippi clay, flies over his left shoulder, he mumbles, "He do thee wrong to take thee out o' th' grave. Thou shalt remain a soul in bliss; but he remaineth bound in upon a wheel of fire, no tears came for thy child. Only darkness and sorrow in a walled prison of green." He pauses to catch his breath, gives the dark sky a quick glance, and continues to dig. "I pray thee Highness, be thou just; let sorrow split my heart or this fool servant shall be a madman." The floating fog moves over and around him like smoke from a hidden fire.

Eleanor and Julius Caesar are inside the Franklin mausoleum. There is a little stone bench made of red Verona Italian marble and various books strewn about the stone floor. Eleanor sits on the Italian marble bench while Julius Caesar corners a mouse. She picks up an old book by Oscar Wilde, and sighs with regret. She looks around and is taken in by a deep wave of confusion when an even deeper feeling of unhappiness engulfs her mind. She says, "Edward, my birthday is just around the corner. Oh, how I do wish you would pull yourself away from your work. We could ride through Oxford and watch the leaves change and the snow fall. Would you come home more often?"

Julius Caesar slaps a claw at the mouse and snarls, but Eleanor doesn't notice.

"Can we go somewhere, Edward? One time, *you and me*, please? Remember in New England when Poppa and Momma gave me a birthday party and you asked me to marry you?" She pauses and takes a deep breath.

Julius Caesar snarls louder.

"Poppa stormed Belladonna with sound and fury when we ran off and took the train to Mississippi. I never told you the truth."

The mouse squeals.

"Poppa never spoke to me again. I miss Poppa. My eyes hurt me all the time. *Parched*," she says earnestly, rubbing at her eyes with balled up fists. In her mind, she hears the *Happy Birthday* song.

The mouse squeals when Julius Caesar kills it. He looks towards Eleanor then walks over to her with the mouse in his mouth. She glances at him, and then he drops it at her feet. Blood runs down both sides of his white face. She smiles with approval, reaches down and picks up the mouse, and walks towards the mausoleum's entrance, steps out and throws it into the night air.

Mordecai is still digging by the moonlight. He's inside a hole. All that can be seen is red-orange, muddy Mississippi clay flying up towards sky. Snow has begun to fall in Saint Peter's Cemetery.

Eleanor gives her hand a light brush against her green velvet cape, trembles, and then walks back into the Franklin mausoleum. She continues to talk to Edward while remembering the past. "Edward, you know if Poppa was alive." She stops and considers. "Poppa never had to whip me but one time. Why, I still have scars on my back. Come to think of it, I wouldn't recognize him now. Would I?" she asks in a cold, pondering voice. She pauses and thinks back, then gives a regretful look out into the darkness before saying, "Poppa ruined my life as a woman, as a wife, as a mother. Ruined. After I left, at dusk one evening, Momma had to do what she had to do. I never held it against her. Poppa was *too furious* to die on his own. They were so good to me. Remember my sixteenth birthday party? I'm having a party soon." Eleanor stops talking and considers for a minute. Her eyes widen. Their center glow with light. She believes Edward is talking to her. "Yes, at Fable Court!" She pauses, blinks twice, and squeals. "You agree? Oh good! I'm one step ahead of you. I've invited Mary and Joe.

I am giving them a gift. You never gave *anyone other than yourself* a gift, did you? I missed their wedding. Layne and I haven't got out much since you left. How exciting for me, a birthday party! Would you come?"

An owl hoots twice.

"I understand. Layne? Mordecai looks after him now. Mordecai is finishing up your wall mosaic. I had Venetian glass sent in from Venice for him to use. He and William fill memory books. You know, my eyes pain my brain. Sometimes Fable Court goes completely dark on me. Doctor Moss says not to worry though. He's down in New Orleans at a clinic on Lake Pontchartrain."

She smiles at Julius Caesar who cuts his eyes at her to let her know he's been listening. He continues to lick blood from his paws. She trembles again. She smiles. She grows nostalgic.

"Remember, New Orleans?" she asks, smoothing down her green velvet cape. Again, the owl hoots twice.

Julius Caesar jumps onto the entrance gate of the mausoleum. He sees the owl still tearing the mouse to pieces. The owl spots the cat and takes up what's left of his find and flies towards a little deserted shed where a gray-headed older man—William Faulkner—is drinking from a whiskey bottle.

Lightly dusted with snow, Mordecai climbs out from the hole he's been digging. "A quarter 'til—time to go," he says, checking his gold pocket watch. He considers the darkness. He stares into a freshly dug grave. "A house divided cannot stand ... nor will any kingdom." He turns and walks back into the shed, changes his clothes, and hides once again behind the oak tree. The snow continues to fall softly. He stands hidden from Eleanor with his hands in his pockets. He watches the owl finish tearing the mouse apart on top of a lightly snow dusted grave site. The headstone reads *Stringer*.

Back in the Franklin mausoleum, Eleanor continues talking and remembering times past. "Edward, do you miss your students? What? The White House?! Oh no, I won't allow it!" She stops talking, gathers her bearings. "Yes, the University of Mississippi—Ole Miss—is not the same without you. I gave the Department of Classics the money you requested."

Outside the Franklin mausoleum, leaves are falling from an old tree. A winter breeze whispers beneath them and then floats them across the graveyard like souls caught up in a tornado looking for rest.

"No one ever comes to visit me. It's so lonely at Fable Court. The only company I enjoy is the Southern light." She stops to wipe her eyes. She smiles. "Come to think of it, William does come around ...

I saved every penny. The land too. Never given away a dime except to Ole Miss." She bites at her bottom lip. She wrings her hands. "I miss the Negroes. They were so much company for me and Layne." She nods off. She closes her eyes before saying from another place and time, "Poppa—I mean, Edward, —no one ever comes except for the cars, and, of course, my dear, old friends from Amherst—Abby Woods, Hattie and Sarah Merrill, and Abiah Root. Thomas has beautiful daylilies in his hand." She opens her eyes and holds herself up straighter like she's expecting an answer.

Still, no answer.

"The leaves have changed. Still, I collect them in Mason jars." She trembles. "Julius Caesar is here. I have a favorite poem. *Read it?*" She gives Julius Caesar a defeated look. "Still, the nights are long and cold in Sardis, you know ... I'm just a needless old woman ending my song who, like a wounded snake, drags its slow length along ... *Edward, would you just hold my hand?*"

She reaches for an Emily Dickinson book of poetry on the Italian marble bench, opens it, and reads aloud, *"There's a certain Slant of light, / Winter Afternoons— / That oppresses, like the Heft / Of Cathedral Tunes— /"* She takes a deep breath. "Edward, I think the Lord is about to call my name." After a short pause, *"Heavenly Hurt, it gives us— / We can find no scar, / But internal difference— / Where the Meanings, are— /"* With reflection, "Edward, I miss Layne. I wish that—He always was such a sweet boy." She sighs. *"None may teach it—Any— / 'Tis the Seal Despair / An imperial affliction / Sent us of the Air— /"* She closes then opens her eyes. "Edward, I do wish you would take the time off to come to my birthday party, I'll get a tree. I wrote and invited Mary and Joe. I still have all those lovely decorations from our travels," she pleads. She hangs her head down, considers, and then says, "Edward, I have the first decoration Momma and I made from baby pink felt with pink pearls, rhinestones, and lavender." She closes then opens her eyes. "Oh, Edward, I may be mistaken all together!"

She straightens her poetry book and reads, *"When it comes, the Landscape listens— / Shadows—hold their breath— / When it goes, 'tis like the Distance / On the look of Death—"* She smiles and pauses then motions for Julius Caesar to come closer. "Edward, why can't we start our story over?"

No answer.

"Come on, Julius Caesar. Time to go home. We have something to do now—make a party. Goodbye Edward—you were always such a good provider. I am sorry, you know," she tells him, ever-pausing for a reply.

Silence.

She looks lost and confused. She begins to trace the cover of her poetry book before throwing it open-faced against the red Italian marble of the mausoleum. She looks at its east wall where Claude Monet's *Lavacourt: Sunshine and Snow* dated 1881 hangs.

Julius Caesar, perhaps in sympathy, jumps into her lap and meows.

Her mood changes. She drifts off into an even deeper state of confusion. She becomes angry. "No words, no words! Hush!" she tells Julius Caesar, switching to another state of mind. "Julius, do you like Edward? *Imagine* a party after all these years. Is that you Poppa, calling me your Daisy? I thought I heard my name. Lavinia, is that you? *Vinnie?*" She looks around the mausoleum. She mumbles to herself while opening her purse. "My eyes are about to quit on me! Oh, dear God, what to do now? How did it get so cold so fast?" She believes that she sees Edward smiling. They are walking hand in hand amid a field of yellow buttercups. In her free hand, she is holding a bouquet of pink-purple heliotrope flowers. She puts on her dark spectacles.

THE SUN'S RAY'S SEEP from the eastern sky into Oxford as Eleanor and Julius Caesar enter Fable Court all dusted with snow. Outside of town an older couple with Alabama license plates are driving along the partially sunlit highway. The car slows to read from a large sign that's posted between two pines. At the same time, they read, *FREE LAND at Number 33 Fable Court—Just for the Asking. Everyone is Welcome! Straight on ahead.* The man flashes the woman a hopeful look. He speeds on ahead.

Inside the Franklin kitchen, the Southern light bursts from a rose-colored side windowpane while Mordecai serves Eleanor and Julius Caesar their breakfast. It has stopped snowing in Oxford. The window has a checkerboard pattern with black and white squares along each side of a large red rose and there is clear glass squares amid its pale blue trim. The kitchen is done in a glistening clean white except for one side that looks Victorian and is trimmed in azure.

"Mordecai, how's the wall mosaic coming along?" Eleanor asks.

"The same—it never changes. I continue to rearrange with Billy's help," Mordecai answers without any emotion in his voice—as if he were dead.

Eleanor catches the coldness in his voice. She gives him a startled look. Julius Caesar struts over towards a silver saucer overflowing with fresh cream.

"Oh, my! Well, I suppose Fable Court will never be the same without Edward here to help us," she says, looking limp. "We had such a lovely visit this morning." She takes in a deep breath and asks, "How's Layne?"

Julius Caesar looks up, whiskers tipped with cream.

Mordecai begins to pour coffee for Eleanor who finally takes some initiative to help herself by steadying her cup for him. He gives her a sad look. "I suppose so. The same—Layne never changes either. He rearranges too. Billy has taught him a lot. He needs you, not Billy or me or an animal."

She catches his look. She becomes defensive and tells him, "Mordecai, don't waste any of this food. Save what's left for our dinner!" She stuffs a biscuit along with a hunk of salt pork into her apron pocket. "You hear me? You can warm up this coffee on the gas top as well. It's too cold for me."

Mordecai nods at her as if his nod were nothing more than a natural reflex that he'd been accustomed to doing for years.

FREE LAND

Chapter 4

BEING FROM SELMA, ALABAMA, where it feels as hot as hell for much of the year, the Reverend Morty Rayborn decided at the beginning of his ministry that he would take his yearly vacation in December. Once, when his wife, Lucy, questioned his December decision, he told her it was easy to get a substitute preacher because everyone needed some extra Christmas money. She agreed, packed her bags, and headed for the car.

When the Rayborns pull into the driveway of Fable Court their idea is to get the free land and go. That's not how it works out—at least not in *that* order.

"LUCY, WHAT DO YOU THINK OF THIS ONE?" Morty asks, pointing to the house. He puffs a cigar while straightening his cowboy hat before he opens the car door.

Lucy gives her road map a firm shake. She folds it and stuffs it in the bend of the front seat. "Morty, you know how I feel about stoppin' at all these hokey road-sign offers. Why, the last one you stopped at— at that Stuckey's Restaurant—we was lost in Hattiesburg or one of the other Podunk towns YOU got us lost in. The one that read, 'Free Florida Orange Juice with the Purchase of a Pecan Praline.'" She begins to smack her gum and talk faster and at flick her cherry-red fingernails. "And we about got slicked out of the car for World War II 1945 bonds—expired no less—, not to mention the indoor *one and only* bathroom was 'Out of Order.' We only found *that* out after we had drunk five glasses of free orange juice, had to go behind the restaurant and pee right there in front of God and everybody."

Morty pretends to ignore her. He wiggles in his car seat.

Lucy takes in a breath of fresh air, fills her jaws, and then releases it into the front windshield. She becomes exasperated, thinking about that trip. Morty become nervous too.

Morty flings her an agitated look before he says, "Now Lucy, don't you start up your naggin' then braggin' how smart you are with me!

All I was tryin' to do was load us up on the Vitamin C!" He takes a light puff from his cigar. "How was I supposed to know that some kid had plugged up the indoor toilet with a *Superman* comic book?"

Lucy smacks her gum wildly. She becomes defensive. "Listen, I ain't startin' nothin' with you. You knew when you married me, I was a straight-A student!" She considers a minute before saying, "I just can't help but ask myself the question a hundred times over *why* I married a man whose idea of a vacation is ridin' from Selma, Alabama, slam down to New Orleans, Louisiana, every year—December to be exact. Dear Lord in heaven, *why* did I marry a man that stops each and every time he sees a *hokey road sign*, no less, or when he *thinks* he's found a free ad-verse-ment!" She pauses. She throws him a regretful look. "Morty, I don't know *why* I let you talk me into gettin' in the car with you again—Sweet Jesus!" She considers her words. "What in the world would our members back in Selma say about you if they knew you had such a *fling* for roadside ad-ven-ture?" She pops her gum twice.

Morty is not moved. He ignores Lucy. His imagination runs wild and takes hold of his reasoning power. He is excited about what *could* happen this time. He knocks three times on the car dash with his right fist. His countenance changes. He smiles and shakes his head. "Lucy,

I got a feelin' about this one. We could very well be on the brink of God's blessin'!' There ain't no tellin' to what we could end up with! The Bible says, 'Eyes have not seen, ears have not heard what He has prepared for them that love and serve Him!'" He slams his fist on the dashboard. He begins to tremble.

Lucy's eyes widen. "Morty, you think this could be what He *has had* in the works for us? Are you tellin' me that we are on the brink or doorstep of all our dreams comin' true? Are our prayers about to be answered in some *strange and mysterious* way? Oh, my Lord in heaven! Could this be the *One* He has been savin' for us?!" she asks, actually wondering.

"And I can quit the ministry!" he beams out. Balls of sweat roll off his forehead onto his face. He takes out a handkerchief and dabs at his face. He wipes a tear from the corner of his eye. He tips his cowboy hat. "Lucy, you know Momma dedicated me to the Lord God one June Sunday morning in Pearl, Mississippi. Always believing He had something special for me to do one day."

Lucy has been through this before. She is not going to be moved. "Lucy, I got a feelin' about *this One*. Better get yourself ready to fly away on *this One*!" she blurts out in a falsetto voice mimicking Morty.

Instantly, he tunes her out.

"Momma said this! Momma did that! Sunday morning. Sunday night. *Who even knows if* your momma was even in her right mind beings, she suffered living with a man who loved the whiskey bottle more than he loved her or loved you for that matter?!"

Morty cuts her a look that would disable a rattlesnake's rattle.

The Rayborns sit in their car a little longer both eyeing the Southern antebellum house in the heavily lightsome style of a century ago. It had once been white on what was one of Oxford's most select streets now encroached and obliterated. A house on its way to a dusty death. Its half-a-dozen columns with their paint now flaking away suggests that houses like people indeed deteriorate if left alone with themselves. The house's salvation is a gated courtyard with a spiked wrought iron fence. Perhaps the Rayborns are wondering if they can enter without an invitation or a key or both. Lucy reaches and pokes at the map while Morty sits back blowing a stream of smoke rings out the car window. He turns and gives her a big smile like he's about to discover buried treasure. She checks her face in the rearview mirror. She applies a fresh red coat of cherry-red lipstick she bought at their Hattiesburg stop at Stuckey's from a lady selling Avon products out of her Cadillac.

They get out of the car and walk to the front door. At first, both try to knock until Lucy wins and makes the first tap. This agitates Morty, so he bends over in front of her and raises his eyebrows. After what seems like an eternity, Mordecai greets them with his grave look before escorting them into the Franklin parlor where Eleanor and Julius Caesar are nibbling at refreshments served on Desert Rose China. Precious art wallpapers the walls of Fable Court. There is a Norman Rockwell oil painting hanging adjacent to a big bay window that the morning's southern light is pouring through.

They sit on the couch. Lucy stands and walks over to the oil painting and reads aloud, *An Old English Christmas These were the Players, 1920.*

"It's a *Norman Rockwell*—an original," Eleanor remarks, looking into her teacup.

The painting has eight English children being led into a room by two other English children dressed as their King and Queen and one small chap standing at attention pretending to pose as a soldier. The King and Queen are being followed by others who are dressed as members of their Court.

"Missy tell me, where on earth did you find such a treasure?!" Lucy blurts out.

"I got it from the artist—where else would I get it?" Eleanor asks her teacup, smiling.

Julius Caesar purrs in his own thoughts.

"Hush up, Julius," she scolds the cat then adds, "Someone must be coming because he always makes the most noise whenever he hears the engine of one of the cars purring outside."

"Missy, yaw'll got any white gloves?" Lucy asks. Morty joins her to admire the oil painting.

Mordecai nods.

"Well, I'll be—a Norman Rockwell. It certainly is nice. How much is it worth?" Morty asks, eyeing the signature.

"Morty!" Lucy exclaims with horror, but to her amazement Eleanor doesn't seem to be the least bit insulted by his question.

"Well, I have known Norman Rockwell for many years. When his Vermont studio burned to the ground back in 1943, I was lucky enough to already have been given this one by him and his lovely wife. No one knows that I have it; otherwise, they'd come and take it away," she tells them.

"It moves me like a good sermon or somethin'," Morty says, looking glassy-eyed.

Lucy rolls her eyes.

"Wonderful! Norman would be pleased by your words because his paintings are rarely seen by the public. I am thankful to have this one to share with the cars," she tells them.

"Tap, tap, tap," echoes from the brass door knocker all through the house from the front door.

"*The cars?*" someone asks.

"Oh yes, that must be more visitors in their cars," Eleanor says, putting her dark spectacles on. "Mordecai, won't you go and tell them to come back later on in the day as we have company right now?"

Mordecai nods and leaves the parlor, walking down a long hallway that has the feel of tunneling underground. Before Mordecai answers the knock at the door, he stops then reaches into an aluminum bucket and brings back an oversized sterling silver spoon and sprinkles a white powder along the base of the wall.

Lucy gives Morty a puzzled look, tilting her neck back while eyeing Eleanor's dark spectacles.

An old grandfather clock is ticking like a healthy heartbeat. The sunlight continues to pour into the parlor through the bay window. The walls are blue. There is more than a slight hint of a Victorian scheme throughout the room. The furniture is skirted. The tabletops are covered with pieces of light green Depression glass. Big Band or

Swing music begins to play from a 1940 RCA Victor console floor model radio. The sofa looks old with its horsehair covering. Its rosewood curves are so worn down that it hardly bears any resemblance whatsoever to those of the human body like it once did when it was new in 1888. Even though the sun is spinning its light through the bay window, the room still has a cold, stuffy, and dead feeling to it.

Eleanor smiles at the Rayborns. "Tell me about yourselves." She sets her teacup in the middle of a pretty little oval doily. "Are you in the ministry or such?"

Morty reaches for a tea biscuit, "Yes ma'am. Got me a little church over towards the Selma and Black Creek Line—right about where Alabama and Georgia meet. Ain't that right, Lucy?"

Lucy flicks at her fingernails. Morty turns his tea biscuit around like he's checking it for flaws. "I'd say it was closer to Selma than Georgia," she says.

"Done," Mordecai says, walking back into the parlor.

Eleanor removes her dark spectacles.

Lucy turns toward Mordecai and says, "Hey, these are the best tea biscuits that I've ever sunk my teeth in! Where in Sam Hill did you get 'em from?"

Mordecai gives her a blank look when she puts an entire tea biscuit into her mouth and chomps down on it like a dog chomping on a bone.

Morty throws his eyes back into his head and gives Eleanor a quick, embarrassed glance.

Eleanor catches his glance and gives Lucy an approving look. "Thank you kindly.

They are right tasty, aren't they?"

The Rayborn's compliments encourage Mordecai's feelings. He cracks a hint of a smile. He finds himself liking this strange woman. He walks over and offers Lucy another tea biscuit from his sandwich tray.

"I had Mordecai get them from *Annabelle's Bakery* in downtown Oxford. Violet helped make them. She's a *special* girl," Eleanor tells them.

Morty sniffs a tea biscuit. "Reminds me of cashews." He clears his throat. "I'll take a swig of that cider myself. If you don't mind, that is."

Mordecai pours him an apple cider and freshens up everyone's cups including Julius Caesar's silver saucer of cream.

"I just love this place. Why, it reminds me of a picture right out of a Christmas catalog. Don't it you, Morty?" Lucy says, looking around the room.

"Why thank you kindly," Eleanor says in a pleasing tone, sitting up straighter in her chair.

Morty looks around the parlor before he answers his wife, "Reminds me of heaven on earth. Yep, sure does—heaven. Never seen such a house like this in all my years in the ministry. Why it's like a page right outta a storybook or something'! Beau-ti-ful in a tempting *and* spooky sort of way. Kinda like the kiss of a forbidden woman!" He pauses and clears his throat once again then mumbles, "Now *that would* put me in heaven all right. Yep, sure reminds me of heaven on earth." Looking nervous and trembling he asks, "Tell me now, Miss Eleanor, how much *land* are you givin' away today?"

Lucy tenses up in her seat.

Mordecai looks around the parlor grimly before leaving.

Lucy sits straighter and listens for an answer. She gives Julius Caesar a quick glance. She cuts her eyes towards Eleanor and Mordecai's way before smiling cynically to herself.

Eleanor catches Lucy's glance at Julius Caesar and ignores Morty's question. "Julius, come here. Reverend, have you met my cat?"

Lucy gives Morty a blank look, turns to Eleanor, and smiles.

Morty stuffs his cigar into the right corner of his mouth. He flicks it with his bottom teeth sizing up the entire situation while thinking about what to say or do next.

Lucy whispers to Morty, "Here we go, Lov-er-boy. I know how these *cat* lovers can be."

Morty ignores her.

He says to Eleanor, "No. I don't think we've met. If you don't mind, call me Morty." He points to Lucy. "And this here's my Lucy."

"Ah," Eleanor says, without any change in her expression.

Lucy whispers, "Drifting and dreaming like a holy rollin' stone…"

Morty begins to wonder if Eleanor even *knows* about the road sign offering the free land.

Eleanor reaches down and picks up Julius Caesar who is wearing a gold smoking jacket with his JC initials monogrammed in red velvet on the collar.

Lucy smiles cynically while taking another sip from her teacup. Morty begins to pat his right foot and flick his unlit cigar faster with his bottom teeth. He gets out a book of matches and lights it.

"All right then—Morty and Lucy." She stops speaking and pats the cat's head. "This is Julius Caesar." She takes a deep breath. "Julius, say hello to our guests."

The cat looks up at Eleanor and meows for a few seconds while seemingly taking part in the conversation.

Eleanor smiles at her guests.

Morty is impressed and asks his wife, "Lucy would you look at that?" He stops speaking for a minute to look at Eleanor. He looks at the Persian cat. "I'll be dog! Shoot! *Excuse me.* That cat is sure right friendly, ain't he? Would you just look at his eyes? Two different colors!"

Lucy cracks, "Lifts me, I mean *us*, up to Paradise all right!"

Eleanor smiles and reaches for a little dinner bell. "He's all I have—you know since my Edward left me. And *Layne*—well, Mordecai looks after him."

Eleanor's words cause stirring in Lucy. "Your old man left, eh? Oh, I hate to hear that!" She stops talking for a second and looks over at Morty then back to Eleanor. "Is that why you are tryin' to get rid of your land—can't make ends meet? Why, my sister, Lonnie Sue, her old man, Cecil, left her for another woman. She had to up and sell everything in her entire house to pay her bills!"

"Mercy!" Eleanor cries out startling Morty.

Lucy begins to think aloud, "Why, I'll break his scrawny chicken neck if I ever lay eyes on him again!" She gives Eleanor a concerned look then says, "Honey, you broke too?"

Eleanor pretends not to hear Lucy and rings the little dinner bell while Morty looks around the parlor. Mordecai walks in with a quill in his hand. Lucy throws Morty a panicky look when she sees the quill.

"Yes," Mordecai says, looking around the room.

Lucy and Morty look at Mordecai and smile cordially. Mordecai looks from Eleanor to Julius Caesar to Morty and settles a hard but sure stare onto Lucy, wondering why he likes this strange woman.

Eleanor puts on her dark spectacles. "Mordecai, would you freshen up our drinks before these lovely people have to go back to their cars?"

Mordecai nods. Lucy gives Morty a catty, "I told you so," look.

Morty ignores her and clears his throat. "Ma'am, how much land you a-wantin' to get shed of?" He pauses to take his cigar from his mouth. Out of habit, he dumps the butt of his cigar into his Desert Rose teacup using it for an ash tray. "We saw the road sign and all.

Matter of fact, that's why we stopped." He considers then asks her actually wondering, "How *else* would we have known to stop?"

Eleanor looks at the bay window and ignores his question. Lucy decides to jump in with, "Honey, why did you say your old man left you?"

Mordecai leaves the parlor.

Lucy and Morty pretend to ignore Eleanor's dark spectacles until Lucy begins to screw one of her knuckles into her right cheek signaling Morty to take note of the dark glasses. He gets her hint, rolls his eyes back at her, and shrugs his shoulders.

Serving as her own witness, she tells them, "Well, he died is all—and left me here... And Layne, Layne's *my* son, you know. We are alone—except for the land that surrounds Fable Court." She looks straight ahead, takes a deep breath, and releases it before adding, "But we—Julius Caesar and I, that is—go and visit Edward every morning unless he decides to break away and comes around for tea before he goes to Ole Miss then on to the White House." She trembles, turns, and asks her cat, "Right, Julius?"

Julius Caesar blinks twice then yawns, letting out a faint purr.

Lucy gives Morty a sharp look. She weaves her fingers and cracks her knuckles before saying, "He died is *all*? I'd say that's a good enough reason to leave as any I've ever heard!"

Morty despises this knuckle cracking habit of hers. It sets off his temper. Like clockwork, he jumps to his feet, and only after realizing that they are not in Selma, Alabama, does he sit down, rubbing at the tops of his legs amid quick and sharp breaths while his face takes on a red glow. "Lucy, you've just got to get on my nerves, don't you?" Morty asks her, pausing to let out a snort before asking Eleanor, "Excuse me Ma'am—you say you got a boy?" He stops speaking and looks around the parlor like he expects to see a new face. "Where's he at?"

Lucy throws Morty a cynical smile. She makes "come here" motions to Julius Caesar with her hands.

Morty squints his eyes. He puckers his lips at Lucy.

Eleanor looks toward the back of the house. "Mordecai looks after Layne." She turns and nudges her cat and says, "Julius Caesar, go and see the Reverend's wife." The cat hesitates. Eleanor persists with, "Go on. Go!" She nudges the cat towards Lucy.

Lucy is curious about the turn in the conversation and asks, "Is Layne lame or what?" Eleanor gives a startled shake in her chair. Lucy smiles at her own question then calls out, "Here, Kitty, Kitty." She turns to Morty and asks, "Julius Caesar was a *prophet* in the Old Testament, right?"

Morty gives her a startled look and the parlor a quick glance over, realizing that something isn't quite right with their hostess. Forgetting his cigar ashes, he takes the last sip from his Desert Rose teacup before standing to go while Lucy waits for his answer. He shrugs his shoulders and scratches his head when Lucy reaches down to the floor and picks up a sand colored mosaic tile, eyes it, then frowns.

He turns and says to Eleanor, "Well, Missy, me and the little lady got to be gettin' on back to our vacation. Come on, Lucy. We appreciate you takin' us in on such short notice. Sorry if we stirred your earthly sorrow. I hope you get rid of that land. Here's my card. You just call me anytime of the day or night for that matter. If you ever want to give us an acre or two, we'll be more than happy to take it off your hands. Give the boy a hug for us and 'hello' to Edward—oops! I mean you have our condolences on his passin' on, I guess?" He looks around the parlor once again and says to his wife, "Right, Lucy?" Although Julius Caesar is sitting in front of Lucy, he has yet to jump into her lap like she had wanted.

"Call anytime?" Eleanor asks them. Eleanor frowns at her cat. She gives the card a quick glance before she places it into her front apron pocket behind the biscuit and hunk of salt pork.

"Whatever you say, Morty. Whatever you say, Morty!" Lucy says then turns to Eleanor and asks, "Honey, you got a powder room so I can freshen up?"

After Eleanor considers her words, she picks up the bell and rings it. Mordecai enters the parlor. She smiles at him and says, "Mordecai, please show Lucy to the powder room."

"Yes, Ma'am," Mordecai says, lingering for a few moments making his ever- presence known to the Rayborns before he says, "This way, please."

"Don't forget to make your wish known to Cordelia," Eleanor tells Lucy who smiles at Eleanor.

Lucy jumps to her feet and follows Mordecai into a long and narrow, half-lit hallway. She notices that the hall has a cloistered feel to it like a monastery. It is made of yellow squared bricks that give the illusion that all who enter are walking underground or tunneling. Lucy looks around. Her mood lightens. When she feels the spirit of the hallway, she cries out with excitement, "Look out, New Or-leans! Hey, Mister, where's the boy that the Mrs. talked about? Is he an invalid or what? Who's Cordelia? Is she the one Edward run off with? Or did she kill her? I wouldn't blame her if she did kill one or both of those heathens! What's all this white stuff along the hallway?"

Mordecai turns his head slowly. He gives Lucy a depressed look, before he says, "Lime." He swallows hard then points to the powder room. He turns and walks away into another narrow hallway. When Lucy goes on into the powder room, she hears him call back, "Cordelia is in the Reading Room."

Once alone in the powder room, Lucy begins to plunder through the medicine cabinet only to find old, outdated medicine bottles labeled, *Charles Edward Franklin.* She opens a little antique pine memory box that is on the top of one of the shelves directly over the toilet. The antique pine memory box has jewelry in it. Her eyes light up as she examines the jewelry. There is a slide bracelet with two slides of pearls and amethysts and a gold necklace with a heart-shaped charm loaded with sparkles of channel set fire, red rubies, and deep, blue sapphires with a brilliant diamond, at least a carat or more, in its middle. She picks out a pair of sterling silver, diamond-studded earrings, rolls off some toilet paper, wraps them in it, and places them into her front dress pocket like a spare hanky.

She stops and considers then says, "No—not this time! This could still be the *One!*" she tells herself, taking the earrings from her pocket and unwrapping the toilet paper from around them. She returns them to the antique pine memory box, flushes the toilet, straightens the hand towel, and then runs out of the powder room and into the narrow hallway towards the parlor to join the others managing to avoid stepping into the lime.

FOUND OBJECTS

Chapter 5

EVEN THOUGH IT IS almost noon in Oxford, Mississippi, a large off-white beeswax candle burns on a milk stool beneath a wall mosaic. In front of the wall mosaic, stands Mordecai Malachi. His eyes—hungry for human touch and companionship—dance to the rhythm of the flickering flame while his fingers trace sand colored mosaic tiles, Venetian glass, found objects and pieces of wood that work together to tell their stories.

"Mordecai? Billy? You there? Come to fetch me?" cries out from the mosaic.

"Be patient, Layne. In time," Mordecai answers. He steps back to consider his work.

There is a closet to the right of the mosaic and a long, narrow window to its left. A glass of water sits on a stool. A bottle of Port wine on the floor stands near a loaf of pumpernickel bread.

Mordecai steps closer to the wall. His vision clouds. He can hear voices in the mosaic.

Mordecai hears King Lear ask William Faulkner, "*What hast thou been in thy life?*"

"*I used to be an honorable devoted servant, proud in heart and mind, that curled my hair, wore my mistress's gloves in my cap as a token of her affection, and slept with my mistress whenever she wanted. I swore oaths with every other word out of my mouth and broke the oaths shamelessly. I used to dream of having sex and wake up to do it. Hard but not cold. I loved wine and gambling and had more women than a Turkish sultan keeps in his harem. I was disloyal and violent. I eavesdropped. I was as lazy as a hog, as sneaky as a fox, as greedy as a wolf, as mad as a dog, and as ruthless as a lion. Don't ever let a woman know what you're thinking. Stay away from whores, don't chase skirts, don't borrow money, and resist the devil. The cold winds still blow through the pear tree in Oxford (addressing an unnamed handsome young boy) my boy, stop that—Let the horse go by least you take a drunken fall and die,*" William Faulkner replies to King Lear.

"*Child Layne to the dark tower came, His word was still—Fie, foh, and fum, I smell the blood of a dead Man*," Mordecai hears someone announce.

"*No words, no words! Hush*," a male voice scolds.

"*He that endureth to the end shall be saved!*" William tells them until the voice from behind the wall mosaic speaks with clarity, "Mordecai, you there? You out there?"

The other voices stop speaking.

Mordecai hears Layne ask, "Mordecai, is that you? Did you bring me any cheese?"

"No words, no words! Hush," Mordecai says, standing back and looking at the mosaic and feeling relieved that the voices he hears in his head from time to time have stopped. His vision clears. The other voice pleads, "Mordecai, I'm *ever* so lonely. It's dark in here. Can I come out? Will you fetch me some eggs?"

No answer.

"*The light is only clouded by the blood of the sun*," a voice says.

Mordecai continues to arrange pieces of Venetian glass, tile, wood, and pottery into a colorful scene while the candle flickers amid the found objects that are held together only by their saintly borders and the voices behind them.

A CAR HORN BLOWS three times. A loud noise is heard within the mosaic like someone falling to his knees.

Mordecai turns and walks away to see why Eleanor didn't ring for him to come to see that the Rayborns and their car got off properly. He smiles when he finds her sitting in the decrepit front porch swing waving good-bye to her guests as if she's known them for years while the Southern light holds up her small, frail body beaming through the crumbling boards of the decrepit swing. He dutifully returns to his wall mosaic and memory books.

In the car Lucy can't resist saying, "Lucy, I've got a feelin' about this One. I can quit the ministry and retire!" She flashes Morty a cynical look.

Morty says, "I gave her my card—you never know—she may call. Yep, you wait and see. I'm tellin' you that the Lord works in *strange and mysterious* ways! You know it?"

"Do I know it? *Do I know it?!* I married you, didn't I? I took God right outta the Sunday morning prayer box on our weddin' day! You don't need *me* to remind *you* what happened on our weddin' night or *do you?!*" she tells him. He ignores her and speeds onto the highway, leaving only a pearly white puff of smoke behind.

In the Reading Room, Eleanor is reading a Jerusalem Bible to herself. She hugs it close to her heart for a few seconds and turns towards a black wrought-iron birdcage in the corner of the room. There is a little bronze plate with the word *Cordelia* engraved beneath its door. Inside the cage sits a bright, red cardinal. Since Mississippi legend holds that cardinals are made for wishing, she mumbles to herself and makes a wish. She throws her neck back and looks up towards the ceiling before crying out, "Oh, dear Lord—please let *somebody* come for my birthday." She raises her hands to her face and with confused eyes she calls out, "Where's my baby? *Laaa-yne?*"

No answer.

She leaves the room with the Jerusalem Bible in her hands all the while looking around for Julius Caesar who is watching Mordecai work on his wall mosaic. Mordecai catches an echo of Eleanor's voice; he stops and leaves the room. Julius Caesar is close at his heels. When they meet in the hallway, Eleanor gives him the Jerusalem Bible and smiles. Dumb with silence, Mordecai takes the Jerusalem Bible and returns to his mosaic.

Once back in the Reading Room, Eleanor stands on a stool and hangs an oatmeal lid string from the ceiling while Julius Caesar watches. Both smile when the cardinal begins to sing.

MERIDIAN

Chapter 6

AFTER A GREAT DEAL OF THOUGHT, Joe and Mary Farmer made Meridian their first home. When Joe accepted a job teaching English at the Vespers High School one month after their November wedding, Mary thought that their eternal bliss would last forever.

Nothing lasts forever though. Not even death.

A FEW WINTER BIRDS ARE SINGING. Christmas music is blaring from an open window of a lilac Victorian house with black trim. A whistling mailman bounces onto the only wrap-around front porch on West Cherry Drive. Cars are buzzing along the street while neighborhood dogs bark at their spinning wheels.

A lighthearted radio announcer's voice calls out, "Gooo-ddd morning Meridian! This is Victor Tyme. Well, it doesn't look like we'll be having a *white* Christmas anytime soon, so all of you out there in radioland and in downtown Meridian will have to settle for the next best thing, Elvis' new Christmas album!" He chuckles a little before continuing on with, "You heard it right—Elvis Presley has done gone and made a Christmas album and WHIT got it first! So, call your friends and sit back and relax while you listen to Mississippi's finest boy sing. All you ladies can sneak me a slice of your fav-or-ite pie—my lips are sealed! You got it *right* with Victor Tyme on WHIT, in Meridian, Mississippi."

The mailman glances at a nearby fresh wash hanging from a clothesline. He stops dead in his tracks, considers for a minute before saying, "Elvis, eh? Well, I'll be dog—a new Christmas album, eh? I'd better call the wife!"

A cheerful Mary Farmer greets him with a smile from behind a screen door while wiping her hands on her apron.

"Can I use your phone? WHIT, eh? That's Doris' fav-or-ite station too. A slice of pie too." Mary says nothing. "Humph! Why, I never heard of *that* before, have you?"

"He does that about twice a week. Oh, sure you can use our telephone." She unlatches the front screen and opens the door. "Come on in. Can I get you some ice tea?"

The mailman considers for a minute and then says, "Sure enough."

She nods at him.

"I could use something cold to wet my whistle." His mind begins to drift, and once again he stops to ponder his thoughts while he rubs his chin with his right hand. "I wonder if that's where *our* pies have been *sneaking* off to. But my old lady can't even drive, not that I know of—that is. I just wonder—Gladys, her sister, drives though."

When the mailman enters the house, Mary points to a small table that has a chair attached to its side with a telephone in its middle. She goes into the kitchen while he dials.

The recorded voice of Elvis Presley, singing the song, *Santa Bring My Baby Back to Me*, blares across the radio waves.

Once in the kitchen, Mary pours the mailman a glass of ice tea. A small puppy is sleeping in a doggie bed between the refrigerator and stove. Her morning dishes are piled up in the sink. Dinner is cooking on the gas top. The smell of salt pork belly and Crowder peas fills the air. She sniffs then walks and opens the window over the kitchen sink and taps the red petal of a poinsettia that's growing in a flower box. She walks back and opens the door of the oven and peaks in at her cornbread. She gives the clock over the stove a quick glance before turning the oven off and lowering the fire beneath her Crowder peas, grabs the glass of ice tea, and leaves the kitchen. When Mary enters the hallway, she sees the mailman sitting half in and half out of the phone table. The radio music is still ringing throughout the house and bouncing back in from the window.

A small, short-haired Chihuahua puppy with a black tail that looks like it has been dabbed once into a bucket of white paint skittles into the room. Mary sits the ice tea down on the phone table, reaches and picks up the puppy. She taps him on the head while her middle finger and her pointer finger tap at his nose. Pulling away from her, the puppy fusses, at her touch.

She smiles when the mailman begins to shout into the receiver, "Listen, Doris, I am tellin' you that *Elvis Presley* is on the radio right now. WHIT. No, I'm not pullin' your leg none! Good Gaw'd a-mighty! What? A *permanent*? Well, then take the cotton out of your ears for Christ's sake! Sweet Jesus!" He chuckles. "You heard me right. Doris, by the way, are you cookin' any *pies* for supper? What do you mean, *'What kind of a stupid question is that?'* Listen, Doris, if you'll stop yellin'. Hell, I was just wonderin'. Can't a husband ask his wife a question?"

Mary raises her eyebrows at him.

He turns his back to her and the Chihuahua. He continues on with, "That's all. Hey, is Gladys over there? In her *car?* Because I want to know, that's why. I got a right to ask my wife a question, don't I? Hello? Hello?" He mumbles, "Hot damn! She hung up in my face!"

The Chihuahua turns, gives him a perky look, and barks, "Ruff." It paints the air with the tip of his white tail.

He pauses then clears his throat before saying to save face, "See you when I get home. Bye-bye. Honey-bunch!" He mumbles beneath his breath, "Women — just try to do them a favor, and you get yelled at and accused of being stupid. Sweet Jesus!"

The Chihuahua barks twice. Mary puts him down on the floor. "Now scoot, Tippy." The little dog attempts to run out of the room. He slips on the floor before running back into the kitchen.

The mailman turns, looking somewhat dazed, and heads towards the screen door. Mary grabs the glass of ice tea and follows him. He doesn't notice her and heads out onto the front porch where Joe is pulling into the driveway in a 1960 powder-blue Pontiac. She reaches and grabs a sprig of mistletoe from a bookshelf with her free hand, and pushes the mailman aside, but not before she shoves the glass of ice tea at him. She rushes out to greet Joe. The mailman shakes his head and comes back to himself. A few squirrels begin to chatter on the front lawn. A neighboring German shepherd runs to join Mary. She holds the sprig of mistletoe over Joe's head. Joe smiles before kissing her on the forehead. When he looks up, he notices that the mailman is walking out of his front door admiring his glass of ice tea grinning like a monkey.

Joe turns to his wife and asks, "Babydoll, what's *he* doing?"

Mary throws the mailman a look before telling Joe, "Called his wife—*Elvis* has a new album."

"What about Elvis?" Joe asks.

Mary looks at the German shepherd and says, "Ladybird, now you git on back home! Do you hear me?" The dog doesn't budge an inch. Instead, she sits down and sets her eyes straight on the mailman.

The mailman takes off his hat, scratches his head, and walks towards Joe. He takes a sip of ice tea before asking, "How's the happy couple?! He turns to Mary and tells her, "*Brisk* tea, eh? Good." Bouncing his head, "Is it Lipton?"

"Worn slam out! And about broke," Joe answers him bluntly, embarrassing Mary.

She turns and scolds him, "Lord, Joe! What'd you have to say *that* for?" Joe ignores her. She turns to the mailman and says, "Why, thank you kindly. You want another glass full?"

The mailman shakes his head no and says, "Nope. I got a letter from Oxford for you two. Got both your names on it. Now ain't that nice?" he tells them before reading, "'Mary and Joe Farmer.' How does it feel to get mail with *both* your names on it?" He chuckles then says, "Other than utility bills!" Mary and Joe stare at him blankly while he appears to be listening to the chimes of Victor Tyme's voice before he says to the sky, "Why, I remember when me and Doris first got married." He turns towards Joe and says, "I want you to know that woman saved every piece of mail that had *both* our names on it for one solid year! Yep—why, she about drove me slam damn crazy!"

Mary's eyes widen.

"Then of all things, she cut out our names in the shapes of little hearts and glued them to the bottom of every damn drawer in the house. Yep! Why do you think I got this job?"

No answer.

"I'll tell you why—to put a stop to the paper and the catalog collectin'.'" He nods at Joe. "Yep. *I* intercept every catalog and add-verse-ment that has *our names* on it first thing in the morning. Yep. I go pretty near thirty-minutes early so I can get a jump on Walter—he's *our* mailman."

Mary gives him a shocked look while Joe looks like he's relating his story.

Joe nods his head, and he starts to laugh. "Shoot! Didn't she think something fishy was going on when she stopped getting catalogs and such?"

"Damn right, she did!" the mailman says, giving them both a sly look. He snorts before adding, "But Walter told her that JFK had done gone and put a stop to all the extra mail stuff—only allowing one or two a month. Heck fire, who'd ever thought that November the eighth day of 1960, would be mine as well as JFK's lucky day?! Then, of all things Gladys went and got Doris into recipe-collectin'. She went and cut out little shapes of various foods to paper a recipe box." He takes a deep breath in to calm himself. "Can you feature that? Can you imagine how I felt every time I went to get a pair of *drawers* and had to look at carrots, celery, and, of course, Irish po-ta-toes? Made me feel like I was on my way to the supper table instead of off to take a bath!"

Joe cracks a smile.

Mary flings out the words, "Lord 'a mercy! Now, who would have ever even thought of such a thing but a genius?!" She appears to ponder the idea over in her mind though. "A recipe box, eh?"

"Did Doris fall for Walter's story or not?" Joe asks, actually wondering.

The mailman chuckles and says, "Yep. Hook, line, and sinker. Yep. Old Walter told her she had a strikin' resemblance to JACKIE K. and all. Well, that's what did it, I suppose." He turns towards Joe and says, "You *know* how vain *some women are*."

Joe gives him a wink and says, "Yep."

Mary gives Joe a hurt look.

The mailman gives a little bow before he hands him the letter. "Here's your letter. Who's it from?"

Mary snatches it before Joe can get a good look. "Why, it's from my Aunt Eleanor Franklin, Momma's only sister. We haven't heard from her in years," Mary says, slapping her right leg in surprise. "Joe, she's the one relative of mine we invited to the wedding. Remember?"

Joe thinks back before he answers with, "Oh, yeah. Babydoll, isn't she the rich old lady that never even sent us a red cent let alone a greeting card?" He considers a minute before he adds, "If I remember correctly—she didn't even respond to our invitation, right?"

Just as soon as the mailman hears Joe say the word *rich*, his ears perk up.

Mary gives them both a defensive look.

"*Rich, eh? She married?*" he asks.

"For both of your information, Aunt Eleanor has been through a lot. Her husband died a *tragic* death of sorts. Nobody knows for sure *why* or *how* he died not to mention what *really* happened to their only boy, Layne. They didn't get along—Uncle Edward and Layne, that is," she blares out.

Ladybird gets up and walks over to the house next door where a lady with a head full of curlers and a small child are sitting on the front porch.

"Why not, Babydoll?" Joe asks her.

The mailman begins to relate to Mary's aunt because he has confused her statement about "only boy" with owning a pet. "Me and Doris never had no kids either. Just as well, I guess. We got us two *fine* bird dogs though," he says with great regret. He stops talking and appears to think back before saying, "Yep! We named them, Jimmy and Benny. That is until we found out that Jimmy was *a she* when the puppies came and had to change *his* name to Jenny. Jimmy and Jenny are the loves of our lives if you want to know the truth about it. Except when it comes to bath time. Hell, they don't even like warm water!" He looks at Mary curiously and asks, "What'd you mean when you said that nobody *really* knows what happened to her *only boy?*"

"I'm not sure. It had something to do with Uncle Edward's feelings about the Negroes though. Seems Layne caught the measles from one of their hired hand's youngins, and, according to the doctor, them measles had an unusual effect on the boy—left him somewhat retarded." She pauses for a few seconds. "And I do declare, it broke Aunt Eleanor's heart slam-in-two!"

"*Somewhat retarded?*" Joe echoes, thinking aloud.

The mailman interrupts with, "You don't say! Well, bless her heart." He considers before saying, "Come to think of it, I've heard that them measles can do quite a bit of harm if they ain't treated properly in the very beginning."

"Then how come I've never heard of such a thing before?" Joe asks them.

Mary and the mailman both glance over at Joe before going back to their conversation. "Yep. That's what they say all right," Mary says. She pauses before adding, "See, Layne, was the spitting image of her

Poppa, Nolan. Great Uncle Nolan." She takes a deep breath and blows it out. She gets a serious look on her face. "She had run away with him — Uncle Edward, that is, when she was only sixteen and left a good life in New England and moved to Oxford, Mississippi, with nothing more than the promise of true love to hold on to." She takes another deep breath. Joe and the mailman move in closer to her.

Joe asks, "I thought your momma was an only child?"

"Momma was adopted into the family. She left home years before Aunt Eleanor did," she tells him. "Their own father pretended that my momma didn't even exist for many years. Eleanor only found out by accident that she had a sister when she was going through some papers looking for her birth certificate before she left their home, Belladonna, to marry. That's what Momma told me," Mary tells Joe.

The mailman shakes his head then asks, "What kind of a man would disown his own child is what I would like to know?"

Joe shrugs his shoulders.

"Well, Uncle Edward loved to read William Shakespeare, and Layne simply could not understand it, not to mention the fact that Layne took straight to the Negro children in and around Oxford. Why, one time, it was told me that he came walking into Uncle Edward's library during a University of Mississippi Board of Trustees Meeting with black shoe polish smeared on his face—looked like a Little Black Sambo shouting, 'Jojo! Jojo!'"

Joe looks shocked by her words and somewhat crazed when the mailman interrupts with, "Great day in the morning! You don't mean it?"

"Yep! On account of him being somewhat retarded, they didn't allow him around the other children or to go to school." She stops speaking and gives them a little laugh. "Now *that's* what embarrassed the living daylights out of his daddy if you ask me. He about beat Layne slam to death and dared for anymore black shoe polish to be brought into Fable Court. Yes, my Aunt Eleanor married a strange bird all right."

Joe backs up and gives Mary a suspicious look.

The mailman is cupping his chin and nodding his head. "Yeah, I heard about things like that, but they were mostly down in New Orleans. If a woman with child is exposed to Voodoo practices, it can affect the unborn child in a peculiar way. Shakespeare was a painter, wasn't he?" Joe's eyes widen. "Why, Doris's sister, Gladys, is just crazy about him." He considers before he asks, "How did you say her old man died?"

Joe throws the mailman an appalled look then says, "Good God Almighty! No! *Shakespeare* was a writer."

"A writer, humph! Like you want to be, right, Joe?" the mailman asks.

Mary ignores them and cuts in with, "Well, if you want to know the truth about it, it was rumored that Uncle Edward was found in one of the bedroom closets of Fable Court in an unrecognizable state!"

"Great day in the morning! Did the retarded boy let loose on him or what?" the mailman cries out.

Joe gives his watch a long look.

"Lord in heaven, no! Why Layne wouldn't hurt a fly. No one knows what really happened. They said it was probably an escaped convict from the Mississippi State Penitentiary Parchman Farm. Had to be." The mailman nods in total agreement with her words. She waits before she says, "My poor Aunt Eleanor was never the same after that. She was the one who found him on her birthday. That was some twenty years ago. It was like something inside her snapped and never grew back." She takes a deep breath, and then continues on with, "When the law got there, they found Aunt Eleanor standing in the front parlor with cake strewn all over the floor."

"*Cake?*" the mailman says.

"Yes. Cake. German chocolate cake, at that. See, she and Layne had baked a cake. They were carrying it into Uncle Edward. They were the ones who found him torn up and in such a fix—a bloody mess was he!"

"Babydoll, why didn't you tell me about all this before?" Joe cries out in a shocked voice.

"Well, if you want to know the truth, I guess I never told anyone about it before until today. I was ashamed of my crazy family. I'm right sorry to put it on you two," she confesses.

The mailman and Joe nod in agreement with her words.

The mailman jumps in with, "I can certainly understand why! What an awful mess! Awe, I mean story." He pats his mail bag twice and says, "Don't be sorry, dear. We *government* men are used to carrying other people's burdens. Hey, that's quite all right! Keep in mind, I *ain't* laughing." He sets his eyes straight on her and gives her a right eye wink.

Joe asks Mary, "Well, Babydoll, are you going to read the letter or stand there holding it all day? I'm ready for my dinner if that's okay with you two." He gives the mailman a hard look as if to say, *Get lost, please.*

He gets Joe's hint to leave and says, "Better be gettin' it on back to the main office. I got mail to deliver, you know. Monday's a big day for the United States Postal Service. Can't let JFK down. It is his first year in office, you know, and Christmas is on her way—just around the corner."

Joe nods.

The mailman shakes his head before saying, "Humph! Black shoe polish, eh? That's a new one on me! I'll be sure and tell Doris and Gladys about this tonight at supper. It'll sure give us something new to talk about." He smiles. "Yep, Santy Claus is right around the corner!" He ponders, and then says, "Bless that old lady's heart. I bet she's a lonely old soul..." He begins to walk off.

Joe opens the screen door and lets Tippy out.

The mailman turns around and says, "Come to think of it, I am gettin' right hungry myself."

Mary asks the mailman, "Are you now? Would you be interested in a piece of peach pie? Made it this morning. Should be cooled off by now. Sweet Georgia peaches!"

As Elvis' voice pours from the radio, a radio announcer's lighthearted voice butts in with, "How about that? Yes, you heard Elvis' Christmas Album first on WHIT in Meridian, Mississippi, with

Victor Tyme. Okay, folks, I'm gonna turn the record over now because my studio is fillin' up with *pies*! Or wasn't five times in a row enough for you?" He chuckles.

Mary and Joe begin to stare down at the letter's return gold leaf stamp which reads, Fable Court.

"So, all you fellows, out there in radioland, I'm with Gene Autry, and all you mailmen out there on this next one, *Here Comes Santa Claus (Right Down Santa Claus Lane.)* Ho, Ho, Ho!" Victor Tyme's voice chimes in.

When Mary and Joe turn to see why the mailman hasn't answered Mary, all they see is his silhouette against the noonshine walking lick-a-dee split down the middle of West Cherry Drive with their little black and white Chihuahua, Tippy, barking nonstop at his heels. After the mailman disappears from sight, Mary and Joe sit in the porch swing while Mary reads the letter aloud.

INCREASE, MISSISSIPPI

Chapter 7

"**B**ABYDOLL, THERE IT IS," Joe tells Mary, pointing to a sign that reads, *The E.W. Hagwood Co., Causeyville, Increase, Mississippi, Established 1942.*

Mary smiles when she sees a smaller sign hanging beneath the first and reads aloud, "Erected 1895."

"Looks like this is the place your Aunt Eleanor wrote us about," Joe observed, and began to turn into the gravel parking lot.

"Sure is. Do we need gas?" Mary asks, eyeing the two-gas-pump general store.

Joe gives the gas tank gage a quick glance before he says, "Nope. Still got pretty near half a tank or more."

"Good. We can run in, get the snuff, and get back on the road, so we won't lose any time," she tells him.

Mary has on an A-line shift dress woven with snowdrops, wood anemones, deep primroses, and delicate sprays of wood violets amid a pale blue floral background. A jaunty, little straw bowler tops her date-brown hair. Tied around the brim of her bowler is a long cornflower-blue ribbon. Poppy colored Espadrilles hug her slim, lean feet. Joe is wearing a casual brown, almost wood-colored, suit with a fresh-picked cotton jersey print shirt, and a navy marble tie dangles loosely from his neck, giving him a relaxed yet stylishly handsome, wholesome Southern look.

Joe puts the Pontiac in park while Mary secures her bowler in the rearview mirror.

"Sounds fine to me," Joe says, opening the door of the car.

Once inside the store, they see three old men playing checkers around an old red pickle barrel. Two are sitting while the one that is standing is coaching one of the men. When Mary walks towards the counter for the snuff, she notices an old lady standing and mumbling to herself. Joe lingers behind to watch the checker game. Mary hears a faint stream of Bob Hope's recorded voice from a little room off to the side of the cash register. The old woman looks up, smiles at her, and then says, "Moorn-ing Honey! What can I do for you today?"

"Good morning! Do you have any R.J. Reynolds Tobacco Company mint-flavored snuff in a glass jar?" Mary asks the old woman who says, "Excuse me, Honey!" and runs towards the music, leaving Mary alone. Mary waits for a short while hoping the old woman will return. Her hope is dashed when from a side room the old woman cries out, "Honey, come on in here for just a minute and see my Christmas puppies!"

"Excuse me?" Mary says.

"I said come on in here and see my Christmas puppies!" she calls once again.

Mary walks towards the old woman's voice.

When Mary walks into the room, the old woman says, "Looky here—these are my Christmas puppies!"

"Oh, my! Look how cute!" Mary observes, eyeing five little poodle puppies that are sitting in a wooden box filled with hay. She looks closer and sees the old lady turn a record album over.

"Honey," the old lady says to Mary, "come in closer and see my babies!"

Mary moves in for a closer look. She bends, pats the poodles, and cries out, "Oh, my goodness! Aren't they just the cutest little things?! Where's their momma?"

"I'm their Momma!" the old lady blares with pride. All the poodle puppies turn their heads simultaneously towards the old woman's voice. "What I meant to say is that their Momma got run over—last week—at pump number two." She looks out the window at the gas pumps.

Mary gasps.

The lady pauses and looks down at Mary's Poppy-colored Espadrilles before giving her a quick glance. "Yep—by a *Northerner* no doubt. Had *I-da-ho* plates. So, I had to take over for her."

Bob Hope's voice sings out from the record player, "*Up on the housetop reindeer pause / Out jumps good old Santa Claus / Down through the chimney with lots of toys / All for the little ones, Christmas joys / Ho, ho, ho! Who wouldn't go! / Ho, ho, ho! Who wouldn't go! / Up on the housetop, click, click, click / Down through the chimney with old Saint Nick...*".

Mary whirls around on the heels of her Espadrilles towards the record player before saying, "Why, I do declare! Do they like that music or not?"

The old woman flashes her a smile as wide as the Mississippi River. "Shoot, yeah! Why, my old man, Fred — by the way Honey, I'm Fern — Fern Price."

Mary nods at Fern twice. "I'm Mary — Mary Farmer."

Fern nods at Mary. "Pleased to make your acquaintance." She stops to gather her thoughts. "Anyhow, like I told my Fred, we just can't give up on them — the puppies — even though we both figured they didn't have a snowball's chance in hell of makin' it without their momma's milk!"

"*Next comes the stocking of little Will / Oh, just see that glorious fill! / Here is a hammer and lots of tacks / Also a ball and a whip that cracks*," Bob Hope's voice chimes out from the record player.

"Yep. We figured they wouldn't make it. Then my Fred's checker partner Booker suggested the music. And by golly, it worked like a charm though it's about to wear me slam out! My Fred can't help you know. Oh! I guess you don't know since you just stopped in and ain't had a chance to meet my Fred."

Mary shakes her head and moves in closer to the poodle puppies who are sitting up and wagging their tails at Fern. She begins to sing along with the record, "...*Ho, ho, ho! Who wouldn't go! / Ho, ho, ho!*

Who wouldn't go! / Up on the housetop, click, click, click / Down thru the chimney with old Saint Nick."

The puppies sit up straighter and hang their chins over the side of their old wooden box, looking out at Mary like they'd known her for years. She smiles down at them.

"See, my Fred is blind and all," Fern tells Mary.

"*Blind?* How does he play checkers if he's blind? Besides, ain't it a little *early* in the day to be up and playin' checkers?" Mary asks Fern.

"Honey, like I told you, Booker is his partner. *Why else* would he need a partner to play a game of checkers? Honey, the word *early* ain't in my Fred's vocabulary! Since he went blind, he doesn't sleep much, says he feels like he's always asleep being in the dark and all the sorrows that come with blindness. Why he and Booker are both *addicted* to that silly game of checkers *and pickles* to boot!" She stops talking and raises her eyebrows towards a door that leads into the room where the men are playing their checkers. "Anyhow, the puppies seem to like the music records. In fact, their favorite is the one we cut over at the church. I'm a member of the First Baptist Church of Causeyville. My Fred, well he ain't a member of anything. Not that I know of, that is. Though he used to try to keep up with the washin' of the Wednesday morning men's prayer meeting breakfast dishes as if a man—any man—could keep a kitchen—any kitchen—properly."

Mary realizes that Fern can go on talking until Christmas, so she interrupts with, "Fern, what time do you have?"

"Pretty near six-thirty or so. Why? Honey, you in a hurry or what?"

"Yeah, kind of. We're on our way to visit my Aunt Eleanor in Oxford," she says.

"Well, why didn't you say so?!" Fern says, looking down at the puppies. "My Fred says I'm going to make *Christian* puppies outta you with the gospel music! That's all right too, ain't it? Do you want your momma to put on *Silent Night* for you so you can go back to sleep or what?" The puppies sit back down, burying themselves in their box of hay. Fern leads Mary back into the front of the store where Joe is watching three old men—Earl, Fred, and Booker—play a serious game of checkers.

"Go on, it's your move, Fred. Let me see what you can do," Earl says, clucking his tongue once.

"*Jump on his King half an inch towards the front row,*" Booker whispers to Fred Price.

"Are you sure?" Fred asks, actually wondering if his partner Booker is on the mark.

"Cluck, cluck," Earl clucks his tongue twice at the checkerboard.

"What do you mean, *am I sure?*" Booker asks Fred about to get offended that his friend doubts his advice.

"Just forget it! I guess I'm just getting too old to think. I was thinking that he wasn't in front row yet. That's all," Fred snaps back at him.

But Booker, being the calm, cool, and collected man that he is, isn't about to get offended and in a soothing voice asks, "Fred, for Christ's sake, now you ain't lost a game in the last year or more. Have you?"

Fred looks over Booker's way and gives a blind grin. "Nope. But you ain't *perfect* either."

Joe looks from one man to the other with pure amazement when Fred jumps on Earl's King in the front row. Joe reaches into his front pocket, pulls out a shiny silver dime and begins to toss it in the air. He drops the silver dime. It rolls beneath the table and lands clear out of his sight. He hunkers down to look for it. Fred offers, "It's over by that corner chair near its left back leg."

And, sure enough, when Joe bends to look beneath the table, he catches sight of the chair's back left corner leg and sees his shiny silver dime.

"How'd you do that?" he asks Fred.

Fred doesn't even bother to answer his customer because now he is giving his undivided attention to his checker game because Earl has crowned one of his pieces.

"Joe, you about ready to go?" Mary calls out to him.

"Cluck, cluck," Earl clucks his tongue twice at Joe. "Pickle?" he offers.

"I'm coming," Joe tells her, figuring some things are better left unexplained.   "Good move, Fred," he confirms. "Much obliged, Mister, but it's too early in the morning for me and a pickle to do battle!"

Fred looks up and smiles at Joe while Earl looks steaming mad and gives Booker a suspicious eye. All three men cry out in unison to Joe, "Merry Christmas!"

Everyone laughs.

Joe walks over to where Mary is putting the snuff into her pocket. He looks up over the cash register and notices a little sign that reads, *God Bless Harry S. Truman* and shakes his head.

"You two look like two peas in a pod! My, ain't you a cute pair? You could be in the movies!" Fern observes in a marveling voice.

Neither one of them gave Fern Price a simple thank you. Mary has reached for Joe's hand and is leading him out the front door of the two-pump general store anxious to get on back on the road to Oxford. After all, it is Christmas Eve.

ONCE IN THE PONTIAC, Mary waves out the window and says, "Look at those beautiful tall, green pines! Ain't they just about the most beautiful trees that you've ever seen?" She scoots over closer to Joe. He punches the gas pedal with excitement.

"Yes, ma'am! They are mighty fine pines. They hold their own pretty near all year round," Joe says, reaching out with his right arm and drawing Mary close to his side.

"Joe, can we take Aunt Eleanor to the picture show as soon as we get settled in at Fable Court?" she asks, reaching to secure her bowler.

"Babydoll, you can't even wait 'till we get to Oxford before you start with your plan-making!" he teases her while trying to light a cigarette with his freehand. "Can you?"

"Oh, Joe—I want to go see that new picture show if it's out yet called Nobody Knows My Name. I want us to cheer Aunt Eleanor up because I can tell from her letter that she is depressed. Maybe Layne can go along. I bet he'd like that, don't you?" she asks, reaching over and taking Joe's cigarette from his mouth and dumping the ashes into the ashtray.

Joe smiles at his wife then says, "Why sure he would! Now, I've heard that that's a right fine picture show. Babydoll, I'd rather see one by that Hitchcock fellow myself."

"Well, I'm not the least bit surprised with that *strange* imagination of yours." She stops to take a deep breath. "I just know how much fun it is to go to a picture show when you can't get out that much. Thought it might be a treat for Aunt Eleanor. That's all."

"Okay, Babydoll, we'll all go if one is showing. I won't say anything to upset your Aunt Eleanor any more than she already is. Deal?" Joe tells her in a promising tone. "What's wrong with wanting to leave my own body and live in my imagination?"

Before Mary can reply a very loud, "Whomp! Thump, Thump, Whomp!" rings out from the front end of the Pontiac.

"Aaaaaaaahahahah! Aaaaaaaahahahah!" Mary screams out while Joe swerves the wheel of the car, almost hitting another oncoming vehicle in the opposite lane.

"Great day in the morning!" Joe cries out.

"Sweet Jesus, Joe! Why I think it was an animal or something?!" she screams, gasping for air. "No, maybe it was a king snake!"

Joe slams on breaks and brings the Pontiac to a stop. Mary begins to rock like a scared child.

Alarmed, Joe cries out to Mary, "Babydoll, if you'll just hold onto your horses! I am trying to stop the damn car! Do you hear me?!"

Mary is looking all around while Joe is shaking his head in disagreement, "A king snake! In the cold of winter? I doubt it!" Concern fills his face. He slams on his brakes once again then he offers, "We may have a hit a deer!"

By the time Joe's words leave his mouth, Mary is jumping from the Pontiac. When he goes to stop her, all he can see is the cornflower-blue ribbon on the back of her bowler streaming in the air behind her while she runs towards whatever they've hit.

"Mary, what in the Sam Hill do you think you're doing? Don't you go and get yourself run over now! We're only ten miles outside of Oxford!" He puts the car in park. "Mary, hold on now! Do you hear me?"

Mary ignores Joe and continues to run down the road.

Joe begins to talk louder and faster to his wife, "Marrr-ry, what in the world will I tell your Aunt Eleanor if you go and get yourself run over ten miles from Fable Court?!"

"Good God Almighty!" Mary cries out and covers her mouth with her hands.

"Babydoll, you're about to scare the holy hell out of me!" Joe hollers while running down the middle of the road after his wife.

"Joe! Oh, my Lord, have mercy! We've hit a *doe*, and she looks like she has a little one in her belly!" Mary bows her head as if to pray.

Joe looks like he's seen a ghost when he asks his wife, "Mary, what do you mean, *'We've hit a doe, and she looks like she has a little one in her belly?!'*"

A tall, stringy man walks up from the woods and in a gruff voice says. "Morning. I'll take it off your hands."

Mary is kneeling beside the doe. A dizzy Joe nearly faints when the fresh smell of blood fills the December air. Mary ignores both men and tries to help the injured doe. She sees that the doe's neck is broken. Blood is pouring from the left side of her mouth. It looks like it couldn't have been far away from the delivery of its fawn because the skin on its stomach is stretched tight. Mary wrings her hands like a frightened child.

"I said, *Morning*," the tall, stringy man repeats himself. Still, no one pays him any mind.

Looking better, "Babydoll, get up off your knees and let me see if I can do anything to help put the doe out of her misery," Joe tells his wife, looking around for a big stick or a rock to kill the doe.

Once again Joe feels a wave of fresh blood flush through his nose. It's so strong that when he swallows, it reeks down into his throat, causing him to clear his throat and spit off to the side of the road. Mary is on her knees hunched down on road with a look of sealed despair on her face.

"Oh, dear Lord!" she gasps, clapping her hands. She reaches over and picks up something that is near the doe's head. The tall, stringy man watches her in an intent manner. His eyes fill with charity. "What's this thing? Why it looks like a piece of wood," Mary observes. "Wonder what it's doing here?"

No answer.

Mary tilts her head a little to the left, at the same time putting the piece of wood into the side pocket of her dress next to the jar of mint-flavored snuff.

The stringy man tries once more with, "How do?"

No answer.

Next, he introduces himself in a friendly voice, "Folks, I'm Newton Knight. I am on my way back to Ellisville, Mississippi." He pauses and then continues, "Yaw'll know it now as *The Free State of Jones*. Yep. I just got back from New Orleans where I done gone and struck up a deal with the Union forces. And if you want to know the truth, I have been on the Leaf River with about 10,000 or more men a-settin' up my own guerrilla army before the CSA, Confederate Southern Army, attacks Soso, Mississippi." He looks down at the dying pregnant doe and gives it his full attention until it takes its last breath.

This time Mary and Joe take notice of him. Joe interrupts him with, "Mister, what in Sam Hill are you going on about? Where did *you* come from?"

"I *said*, I am Newton Knight. I am on my way to Isaac Anderson's place first. He wrote me down in New Orleans and offered me a room in his guest house. He wrote there is a little elementary school across the street from his place. He said that I can sit on the front porch and watch the children play. Said maybe that would ease my nerves," he tells them in an exasperated voice that carries over into his face, causing all of his facial muscles to twist and turn into knots.

After hearing his exasperated voice, Mary takes her eyes off the dead animal and glares suspiciously at him. She asks him, *"Aren't you already dead?"*

Newton Knight is alarmed by her question, grabs at the center of his chest, and jumps back like her words have burned straight through to his heart before asking, "Ma'am, is that what they say?"

Mary remains down on her knees. "Yes. If my memory serves me correctly, you were murdered about 1880 or so in the Anderson's guest house by a Confederate officer that was sent to capture you."

Newton Knight fans a fly away from his face. His eyes fill with sorrow then light. His face becomes more strained.

She gasps.

Joe says nothing. He's not as sensitive to the tall, stringy man as Mary is.

"I've even seen your bloodstain on the dining room floor where they say you fell after he shot you. Why yes, yes, yes, I surely have! Your bloodstain on the floor is still trying to offer life but marred and resigned to its fate of death like this here doe's is ," she tells him in a marveling voice. Mary takes a deep breath and confirms who he is with, "I *do* recognize you from a picture in the old Anderson house that hangs in the dining room beside the stained-glass window that I remember looking out of and seeing that spire of a little white church with my own Daddy, Fenton, before he died the sixth day of October last year from smoking cigarettes and drinking whiskey and beer since he was five years old."

Newton Knight crosses his arms, stands straighter, and gives Mary a pleased look perhaps because she remembers him from his picture.

Joe is neither pleased nor impressed with the conversation. He yells, "Mary! What are you going on about?"

"Well, it's true. All I said is true. He must be a *ghost*," she tells Joe, getting up off her knees. There is nothing she can do for either the doe or the unborn fawn. She faces Newton Knight and asks an accusing question, "You led the deserters, didn't you? That's why the army was able to capture Ellisville."

Joe looks from Mary to Knight and wonders if the poignant smell of the doe's blood has made him have thoughts that have taken over his imagination. He thinks that maybe neither of them has ever even said such ridiculous things let alone that they may be conversing with a ghost. He sees a dark cloud hovering above them amid the early morning light.

Knight spits out the words, "That Confederate officer shot me in the heart! And when they take your heart from you, you ain't worth a hill of beans in the real world." He stops speaking, considering his next words, "Or in any world."

Mary blurts out, "*You are* the farmer turned soldier who first married a Negro girl, aren't you?"

Joe throws Newton Knight a shocked look.

Knight stands back and eyes the dead animal. He doesn't answer Mary.

The more Newton Knight considers what Mary has told him, the more defensive he becomes. "If there had been a *Free State of Jones*, Ellisville would have been the Capitol. I *had* to take to the tall pines and the deep forests of Jones County with my men all because of the planters' war—former slaves. We aren't deserters like they say. So, I'll answer you: Hell no!" He points towards the sky. "God as my witness, I ain't never been no outlaw, let alone a turncoat!"

"Oh, my! Why, I'm sorry to be accusing of you then," Mary tells him.

"After all their condemning, I heard that pretty near a 100 citizens of Ellisville and Jones County had done gone and petitioned the state government to have the name changed to Davis and the county seat to Leville, both being right near Antioch and Mars Hill, if I ain't mistaken. I never knew why," Knight tells them, looking hopeless, but not entirely helpless.

"*Antioch?*" Joe asks but didn't get an answer.

"I will tell you why. They all wanted to put the hateful memory of *The Free State of Jones* behind them. Listen, it was one of your very own kin, Ethel Knight, said that you deserted because you thought that your second wife was having an affair," Mary tells Knight. She stops talking and considers for a moment before she asks him, "Is it true or not?"

"Hell, no! I had to control the government under the federally imposed martial law and Reconstruction. Folks had ought to have left my wife out of it!" Knight blares out with great anger.

Mary is not moved by his words.

Joe rolls his eyes in disbelief.

She asks, "Then if you were in complete control, where's your faith in God? Mister, you have no peace. Otherwise, you'd not be here."

Joe throws Mary a shocked look.

"I told you that I am makin' this trip from New Orleans to visit my friend Isaac Anderson! Don't ask me too many questions!" Knight yells out at Mary, getting back to his original train of thought.

Joe has had enough of the entire situation, so he says, "Cooter Brown, listen here, now if you want to go and get drunk this early in the morning and hide behind pine trees on the highway, that's your business. The same goes to what you choose to go on about to perfect strangers is, but don't go and tell my wife that she's asking you too many questions because you are the one who stopped and started up with your crazy talk and storytelling."

Mary is upset at Joe's words, so she stops her husband by gently putting her hand over his mouth. "Joe, please don't say any more to him. He has suffered enough." She pauses and then with tear-filled eyes asks, "Can't you see that he is all alone? That he's searching for something?"

Joe looks at his wife with disbelieving eyes. Newton Knight is staring cold and hard at them. He asks, "What's today's date?"

"It's December 24, 1960, one day before Christmas. You got anyone to spend Christmas with?" Mary asks him.

Knight says, "Nope," and sets a heavy stare on her.

"Then you are welcome to join us at Number 33 Fable Court in Oxford later on tonight if you like," Mary offers, feeling the weight of his stare.

Joe sees the dark cloud that has been hovering above pass over their heads.

With Mary's kind words, Knight nods. The early sun is rising in the eastern sky. Then, like a gentleman, Knight reaches down and picks up the dead animal, turns, and walks back into the woods.

"Bless his heart," Mary observes, watching Newton Knight disappear out of sight.

"Mary, do you realize just how ridiculous *you two* sounded? *Ghost?* Strange. Pure strange. Will you look at the front end of our new car? It's torn slam up! I'm a good-a-mind to call the law," Joe says, looking at the front end of the Pontiac.

"Joe, look! Across the road—in the distance!"

"Mary, what is it now?"

"Look, look, look!" she shouts.

Joe shakes his head to clear it.

When they both turn, they see a seven-point buck standing behind a barbed wire fence watching and listening amid the landscape of an empty field. The buck turns his head to the side. He then jerks it backward and forward in midair to signal them that all is well between him and them. He bows, and with the speed of a hunter's arrow, the buck soars like sorrow's first tear into the Southern light.

The Farmers get into the Pontiac and drive on to Oxford.

"LET'S LOOK FOR the Faulkner place. We should be pretty close," Mary tells Joe.

When Joe reads a sigh that says, *Oxford,* excitement wells up inside him. He soon slows the Pontiac down at the bend in Garfield Road.

"There it is! Look! Rowan Oak!" Mary shouts, pointing at William Faulkner's white-columned, antebellum house.

Sights and spirits from another time are felt, imagined, and seen by Joe amid the grounds of Rowan Oak. Although he can only see it from the road, it's evident that a man's face is looking out from one of the rainbow-hued, Depression glass windows. The house and people along on their drive resemble the fabled schoolteachers, storekeepers, ancient maiden aunts, whatnot salesmen, iron-willed matriarchs with their daughters and sons and children, hotshot lawyers and honest-john businessmen who hunt in the fall, and the dreamers who never stopped dreaming in Faulkner's fictional Jefferson, Yoknapatawpha County.

"I'm going to be disappointed if we don't get to meet Mister William Faulkner and his wife, Estelle, aren't you?" Mary asks Joe.

Joe doesn't hear her. His imagination grips his mind more. He sets his eyes on a sign that reads *No Trespassing* before he replies to Mary's question about the Faulkners. "You bet I'll be disappointed! Mary, did you know that William Faulkner once lived on South Lamar Street where he spent a lot of time with his grandparents?"

Mary says, "No."

"He went on to live on the Victorian hilltop "Duvall House" on University Avenue. That's where he wrote his most famous short story, *A Rose for Emily*, and that steamy novel *Sanctuary*.

Mary promptly asks, "How do you know so much?"

Joe jerks his neck back and cocks his head towards the left side of the car before confessing, "I read up on him last week. I'm ready to discuss some of his books."

"Well, good for you! You can just tell him about our paths crossing with Newton Knight if we run out of things to talk about." Mary stops talking and gives a shrug before saying, "Look Joe, the sun is about to be in full esteem over Oxford."

A sign that reads *FREE LAND at Number 33 Fable Court—Just for the asking. Everyone is Welcome! Straight on ahead keep driving!* comes into focus for all who drive by it to see.

"What in the world does your Aunt Eleanor mean by putting up such a sign?" Joe asks.

Mary gets an uneasy feeling in the pit of her stomach. She begins to rock in her seat.

Joe puts his arm around her.

She replies, "I don't know. I simply just don't know. Joe, what do you think the purpose of that *Free Land* sign is?"

"Your guess is as good as mine," he replies

"I guess we'll find out the answer to that soon enough. She's probably confused or depressed, so for the time being, let's not mention the sign," Mary says to Joe before she pauses to collect her thoughts. "Okay?"

"Babydoll, if she needs our help, I think we should reach out and help her," he answers.

Mary takes note of his words and shakes her head. "I guess you are right. Look at the how beautiful the rising sun is over Oxford."

"Babydoll, it's pretty all right," he says, taking his arm from around her and gripping at the steering wheel.

She nods.

"This is Garfield Road for sure. Where is Eleanor's place?" he asks, lighting a cigarette.

Mary looks ahead then cries out, "Right there!"

Joe takes a long draw from his cigarette and pulls the Pontiac into Fable Court where Southern light is penetrating through Eleanor Franklin's decrepit wooden front porch swing while it moves amid the North wind's winter breeze. Although the house appears to be empty, it has a sense of magic about it. December morning's dew sparkles and glistens gemming up the green and brown ivy that's spiraled around the front porch's pillars.

With great enthusiasm Mary asks, "Joe, look at the trees! What do they remind you of?"

He gives Mary a puzzled look then says sarcastically, *"Trees? And you?"*

Mary is taken with the way that the trees are planted around the front of Fable Court that she doesn't even catch Joe's sarcastic remark.

"The trees remind me of old-timers talking."

"Talking about what?"

"Of years gone by," she tells him.

"They are life-like all right. Why, they do look like they might be having a conversation amongst themselves," Joe agrees with her.

Mary cocks her head to the left to listen giving the trees a suspicious look.

When the Farmers get out of the Pontiac, they stop and look at the land surrounding Fable Court. Joe pauses and slaps the dent in the front end of the car. He shakes his head yet says nothing as enough land for an entire city fills his eyes.

Mary's eyes widen, "Joe, if the "Free Land" is anything at all like this, I want it! Look at how beautiful the grass is—emerald green—even in December," Mary says and they exchange smiles.

"Babydoll, what do you say we pack up and move to Oxford?!" Joe cries out.

It is Eleanor Franklin who appears on the other side of the front door and says with an old voice filled with a new energy, "My land sakes alive! Children, get on in here and let me look at the both of you!"

At once, Mary and Joe catch her excitement and smile.

"Merry Saturday before Christmas!" Joe says, clapping his hands once in midair.

"A merry Christmas Eve to you, too!" Eleanor says with glee, looking more cheerful, and, truth be told, younger.

Mary realizes that Joe and her aunt haven't met yet and introduces them, "Aunt Eleanor this is Joseph James Farmer—my husband. Joe, this is my Aunt Eleanor Franklin." She gives him a quick wink before saying, "Everyone calls him Joe."

"Pleased to meet you ma'am," Joe says and offers his right hand to Eleanor.

Her eyes fill with tears. She extends her arms to him. "Joe, let me hug you! Oh, my, it's *so good* to see some family—blood kin! I had lost hope that I would see anyone I knew ever again. God has smiled on this old woman and answered her birthday prayer!"

Joe bends, letting Eleanor hug him. Mary and her aunt embrace. When the greetings are over, everyone walks into the Fable Court where Mordecai Malachi is standing close by looking as grave as ever.

Eleanor announces, "This is Mordecai Malachi. He looks after me and Layne. He is from Germany." She waits a minute before she says, "Mordecai, take the children's bags and put them in the front bedroom right next to your writing room."

He raises his eyebrows, but doesn't say a word, which leads Mary and Joe to believe that his English may be weak. They nod at him. He dutifully obeys Eleanor's orders. Mary doesn't wait for them. Instead, she walks ahead like she knows where she's going. Suddenly she shouts out, "Oh, my Lord in heaven! Why, if this isn't the most glorious Christmas tree that I have ever seen in all my born days, I don't know what is!" She slaps the top of her legs once then adds, "Joe, get on in here quick and see if what I see is for real! Or if I'm in a dream, wake me up!"

Silver Bells is playing from a Victor Talking Machine.

Joe gives them both a half grin and walks into the parlor to see a glorious balsam tree that reaches high to an eighteen-foot ceiling. It is bare. The room is furnished like a Victorian "little room," with furniture dating back as far as 1860. The wallpaper has extravagant fringed borders dotted with bits of gold that glisten around the room reflecting simpler though elegant times.

"Where in Sam Hill are the ornaments?" Mary asks her Aunt Eleanor in a shocked voice, eyeing the tree.

Eleanor is softly singing along with the talking machine.

Mordecai puts down their bags and stares into the Christmas tree and mumbles, *Tinker Bells*.

Joe looks around and sees eighteenth-century Christmas illuminations that Eleanor has somehow preserved. As a schoolteacher, he knows that they were originally the only teaching aids used by the Moravian Church. He admires the pictures painted on thin paper that are in front of lighted candles. Even though it is still early morning, they become translucent when the light shines through them. He and

Mary both raise their noses and get a whiff of freshly baked bread as the song *Santa Claus is Coming to Town* fills Fable Court.

"Have you been good?" Eleanor turns and asks Joe.

He nods at her. He smiles over at the Christmas tree, claps, and shouts, "Oh, it's real all right! Babydoll, you aren't dreaming!"

Mordecai turns and marches out of the parlor like a German soldier.

"Well, my dears, I've left most of the decorating to you two. I've invited Mr. William Faulkner and his lovely wife, Estelle, over to Fable Court tonight to decorate the Christmas tree with you," Eleanor tells them, pausing to collect her thoughts. "He accepted my invitation, but Estelle didn't. She doesn't go out on Christmas Eve like William does."

Eleanor's words excite Joe who smiles. Mary gives them a frown.

"Great day in the morning! Babydoll, how about that—he is a-coming!" Joe tells Mary who mumbles, "He is going out on Christmas Eve *without his wife?*"

Joe's words tickle Eleanor, and catching his energy, she quivers with excitement.

Mary turns and offers her a hug before she says, "How wonderful! Oh, I am so excited that I can hardly wait!"

Eleanor whispers to Mary, "William Faulkner is only a man, isn't he?"

Mary frowns.

Joe looks around the little room then down the hall and wonders why Mordecai marched off.

"I'm so glad to see you two, but my dear Mary..." she begins, reaching into her apron pocket for a pair of spectacles that hold black lenses instead of clear ones.

Mary frowns when Eleanor puts on the dark spectacles.

"I've about lost my vision. I made up my mind not to let it get away from me until I saw you both and had my eighty-eighth birthday party tonight," she tells them.

Joe stares at her dark spectacles. He turns and walks around the big Christmas tree.

"Aunt Eleanor, why whatever do you mean? I thought you were seeing a doctor down in New Orleans."

"You mean, Doctor Moss? Oh, yes, and I do enjoy the ride down there on the train—with all the people. Yes, I just love seeing their silhouettes on Lake Pontchartrain when we ride over the water."

Mary interrupts with, "What on earth has happened then?"

Joe gives them a glance before leaving the parlor.

"Doctor Moss says that there is not one more thing he can do. I feel like there's a funeral in my brain when the light slants and hits my eyes at times. Especially when I'm with Edward," she confesses. Her mind seems to drift off into another room.

Again, Mary frowns.

Joe interrupts them from another parlor with, "Look here at all these fine decorations! Are they for the tree? How'd you get that big tree into Fable Court anyway?" he calls out.

Even though Eleanor's mood is lifted, Mary can see that her aunt is in worse shape than she had thought. Together, they walk towards Joe's voice.

Once in the other parlor Eleanor says, "The tinsel is from the 1800s—a gift from my mother" and turning towards Mary, "and your grandmother. Many of the ornaments are from the royal weddings that we attended when I was young. Some are faded, but the memories are still in my mind waiting to be called up again."

"Memories are never lost, you know," Mary interjects before adding, "They fade into some dark corner of the mind and wait for us to call them up again. When we don't, they come out when we least expect them to and can *oh so surprise us!*"

Joe smiles at Mary's words, and then holds up an ivory star. "Mary, will you just look at this star? I don't think I've ever seen anything like it before. He turns and asks Eleanor, "Where'd you get it?"

Eleanor looks interested in the star.

Julius Caesar, who has been dozing on a settee, awakens, stretches out, and then struts over to Eleanor, ignoring Mary and Joe.

"That star is carved from pure ivory. Why, one of Edward's favorite writers, Ernest Hemingway, sent it to him from Africa when he was reporting, if I'm not mistaken," she tells them, reaching down to pick up her Persian cat.

"Ernest Hemingway, eh? Well, now if that story doesn't take the place of a birthday cake, I don't know what else will!" Joe says in a disbelieving voice.

Mary gives Joe a sharp look and moves closer to her aunt.

Eleanor is outwardly unaffected by Joe's words and lightheartedly says, "I had the tree brought in from Ole Miss. It cost me a pretty penny." She lowers her voice to a whisper, elbows Mary, and whispers, "Did you get my glass of *mint-flavored snuff?*"

Since women don't usually partake of tobacco openly or in front of men, Mary answers her aunt with, "Oh, yes! I'll give it to you later.

It's in my pocket." Mary reaches over and taps Julius Caesar on the head, noticing his colorful mismatched eyes of blue and yellow.

Joe begins to stare at the cat but soon sets his eyes on Eleanor's dark spectacles.

"We have a little dog named Tippy back in Meridian. A Chihuahua. Our postman is looking after him for us," Mary tells her aunt.

Eleanor smiles at Mary then to Julius Caesar before she places him on the floor.

Julius Caesar responds with a pleasurable purr.

Mary looks down and sees that the cat has a wristwatch strapped around his neck instead of a collar.

Eleanor removes her dark spectacles before calling to her cat, "Come here, Julius Caesar."

The cat struts regal-like towards her. It is sporting a tailored white Christmas-like coat that fits him snugly with the gold letters JC monogrammed across each side of his back.

"Why does Julius Caesar have on a fur coat?" Joe asks.

"Because he's right cold-natured," Eleanor replies.

The cat begins to purr and rub against Eleanor's leg.

"Oh," Joe says, nodding.

"Aunt Eleanor, why does Julius Caesar have a wristwatch on his neck?" Mary asks, taking hold of Joe's arm and pointing at the watch.

"Because that's what I bought him for Christmas."

"Why a wristwatch?" Joe asks.

"Well, if you must know, Julius Caesar is very impatient about things. So, I figured he could learn more about waiting on time if I bought him his own neck watch," she confesses.

Joe smiles.

She gives him a hard look before lowering her voice to a more serious tone and saying, "Mordecai can set the alarm for him if he has something pressing."

Joe gives another quick glance towards the narrow hallway to catch a glimpse of Mordecai with his ear pressed to a door and says, "Well, that sounds like good enough reasons to me!"

Mary smiles when she hears Joe's words to her aunt.

Julius Caesar meows, glancing at Mary then back to Eleanor before stretching out like a king.

Joe asks, "What does Julius Caesar want now?"

Eleanor raises both hands and gives the sky a wave before saying, "Oh, never mind him! He just wants his caviar. He saw me bring it in yesterday. I ordered him a jar of red caviar from Iceland especially for the holidays. He can wait and eat it with the rest of us!" She reaches for the cat.

Mordecai enters the parlor with Mary and Joe's bags.

"Of course, he can! So, let's get started," Mary says, looking around the parlor and feeling anxious.

Once again Eleanor tells Mordecai, "Kindly show my birthday guests to their bedroom."

Mordecai nods. Mary and Joe follow him down the narrow hallway that has the feel of a tunnel deep within the earth. As Joe watches Mordecai, he begins to wonder where Layne is.

"What's that white stuff along the wall?" Mary asks.

"Lime," Mordecai replies, by now knowing that every visitor to the house will ask.

"Lime?" Joe says.

Mary shrugs.

Mordecai nods.

When they enter their bedroom, their eyes lock. Their hearts connect. Joe steals a kiss while Mordecai arranges their bags in a circle before he says, "Follow me."

No one mentions Layne while they walk single file into the Franklin kitchen and sit down to a table set with a breakfast fit for a king.

WINTER PEACE

Chapter 8

LATER THAT DAY Joe, Mary, and Eleanor take an afternoon ride in the Pontiac across the Ole Miss campus. A light wintery haze lingers in the sky. It feels like it might snow. Joe parks the car, and then everyone gets out to walk around the campus.

Eleanor becomes excited when she points at some old buildings. She trembles. "Did you know that in 1862, after the Battle of Shiloh, those buildings over there were used as a hospital for the wounded?"

"No," Joe and Mary answer in unison.

Eleanor gives the buildings an admiring nod. She points and says while shaking her head, "Well, my dears, following the Battle of Shiloh, when Confederate Troops retreated to Oxford and the

University of Mississippi campus, the Lyceum Building was used as a hospital for the wounded Confederate soldiers. It was later that same year when after the Battle of Corinth that Ulysses S. Grant sent troops to occupy Oxford as well." Eleanor pauses to wipe a tear from her eye. "Grant used many of the university's buildings. It was told me that 700 men—mostly Confederate troops—were buried here. Yes, many souls were lay to rest—so they say—over there. Mississippi legend has it that in December some of the souls of the wounded wander back South in search of freedom from their unrest. It was in late August of 1864 when the Union forces lead by General A.J. Smith burned much of the town for a "goodbye gift" that life, and perhaps, time, stood still in Oxford. On Christmas day in 1862 General Grant and his troops left Oxford and winter peace, such as it was, was felt on the campus."

Joe and Mary exchange glances, perhaps thinking of Newton Knight before turning their attention to the Greek Revival Lyceum Building.

In her mind, Eleanor sees Ulysses S. Grant, Commanding General of the Union Army troops, conferring with President Abraham Lincoln over their victory strategy over the Confederacy to win the American Civil War. She sees enemy troops with jagged knives slash, stab, rip, and cut the flesh of the near dead Confederate Soldiers then with a morbid, masculine cheerfulness thrust them into fire pits. Some dead. Some near death to die alive. Blood gushes from eyes that are being gouged out then discarded like bloody daises into a summer field of smoldering broom-like straw or near dead December grass. She sees sticks being poked into the ears of the wounded until they vomit, and their bodies tremble like virgins being raped before they are thrown into the pits of fire. Eleanor screams in the blank of her mind imagining the wartime slaughter of the American Civil War.

Mary eyes two small Confederate flags flanking a monument then asks, "Why is there only one monument if hundreds of soldiers were buried here?"

"Why is there but one lonely grave marker?" Eleanor replies, her mind slowly returning her to Oxford.

"Yes. Where are the others?"

"Well, around the turn of the century workers on the University of Mississippi campus were cleaning up the cemetery and removed them. When they went to replace them, they got confused and didn't know which marker went where. My dears, like many of us, they were never able to make a wrong a right; I guess you could say."

"Do tell," Mary commented.

While Eleanor points, she says, "Yes, my dear Mary, it was the Daughters of the Confederacy that saved the day by erecting this one stone monument and that brick wall over there ... lest we forget our dead ... Yes, lest we forget our dead."

Joe turns to face Eleanor and asks, "Have you ever heard of Newton Knight?"

Eleanor's lifts both arms in the air and says, "Why, of course I have! Folks say that his soul has never made peace with itself. When he appears, he often tells folks that he's on his way to visit a friend in his hometown of Ellisville." She drops her arms back to her sides. "Legend has it that if he talks to you, that you will prosper in Mississippi. Why do you ask of his soul?"

Mary gives Joe's elbow a tight squeeze serving as a hint to keep quiet about what or who they saw earlier on the highway. They lock eyes and their minds meet. He gets her hint and says, "Oh, I just reckon that we young folks are just looking for someone to talk Mississippi history to is all."

"There is nothing historical about a soul searching for peace," she tells them in a stern voice then with a shout, "Be it dead or alive!" She shakes her right fist at them.

Joe feels Mary place something in the palm of his hand. He looks and sees a piece of wood.

"Newton Knight is said to have had a kind heart that leads his wandering soul to do deeds and such," Eleanor says. She considers her thoughts for a moment, draws her neck back, and looks Joe straight in the eye before saying, "The kind of deeds most people let pass by without a thought in the world."

"Sure enough?" Joe comments.

"Whatever do you mean?" Mary asks her aunt.

"Deeds that connect the living to the afterlife."

Joe says, "Sounds mysterious to me."

Eleanor offers a weak smile while looking across the campus. She remembers Edward. She closes her eyes and tilts her head to the right, and when she opens them, she says, "Oh, my! How Edward loved this campus even more than he loved us."

Eleanor's words are upsetting to Mary, and with hopes to cheer her aunt she asks, "How is Layne?"

No answer.

"Hey, while we're out and about, how's about showing us that free land that you mentioned in your invitation?" Joe blurts out.

Mary watches her aunt's reaction to their questions and sees that she is bent on ignoring both questions, Eleanor looks down at her watch. "Oh, my! Do tell. Why it's pretty near five o'clock. I suspect that we'd better be heading on back to Fable Court, don't you, children?"

Joe raises both eyebrows and watches Eleanor brush an amethyst and blue topaz collar broach with her right hand. Mary observes her aunt's mood change and realizes that something may be wrong with her mind. Joe asks her once again, "Hey, I said, while we're out and about, how's about showing us that free land that you mentioned in your invitation?"

Mary elbows him and saves her aunt's feelings by coming to her rescue with, "What? Pretty near five o'clock! Oh, my! We'd better be a-headin' on back to Fable Court; that's for sure."

Eleanor gives Mary an appreciative smile. Mary moves closer to her aunt then turns to Joe and asks, "Isn't that right?"

Joe realizes that it's two to one or perhaps three or four to one if he counts Mordecai and the Persian cat. Now he's wondering if Layne will show up, so he asks, "Eleanor, did you say that Mordecai takes care of Layne?" He stops talking and considers for a minute before he asks her, "Do you think that he'll come meet us later on tonight?"

Eleanor looks uncomfortable and reaches into her purse and pulls out her dark spectacles.

Mary throws Joe a hurt look.

Eleanor puts on her dark spectacles.

Mary sighs as Joe catches her look.

Eleanor answers him with an uneasy, shaky tone in her voice, "Perhaps he will." She appears to stop and think about his request. She cups her chin with her right hand and closes her eyes for a minute before continuing on with, "You know Layne was never the same after the measles. I didn't know *what* to do. From the beginning, I couldn't tell Edward the truth, but he was a smart man and figured it all out anyway..." She stops to gather her thoughts. "The land, yes, it is "free" just like the sign reads. I want to save your wedding gift until later because I'm not sure how much land I want to give to you two. Laurel Stringer, my lawyer, has been helping me work it all out on paper." She glances back down at her watch. "And, besides, Mr. Faulkner will be at Fable Court at seven-o'clock. We must head back." She turns to Mary for some assurance and asks, "Don't you think?"

Mary nods but doesn't speak.

Eleanor turns and walks towards the Pontiac mumbling words that they've never heard before. Mary realizes that her aunt may have nothing other than a story to offer them, so she turns to ask Joe, "What to do now?"

Joe sees how feeble Eleanor is, and as if her dark spectacles aren't enough, she begins to wobble. He is filled with compassion for Mary and her aunt.

"Babydoll, don't you worry about a thing. You hear? We'll just let her do it all the way she wants to," he tells Mary with a right eye wink.

Wobblingly, Eleanor opens the front door of the car.

Mary looks worried and asks, "Joe, where do you suppose Layne is? Is he *really* somewhere in the house, or is her mind so bad and she *thinks* that he's with Mordecai?" She pauses and tries to figure out where her cousin might be.

Joe shrugs when Eleanor cries out from the front seat, "Come on, children, let's go! It's almost my birthday!" She gives them a thirsty look and taps her collar broach once with her right pointer finger.

Joe and Mary get into the car and drive off with thoughts racing between them faster than the Pontiac could ever go.

THE MOOD OF THE EARLY NINETEENTH CENTURY when Mississippians favored the frontiers is felt along Oxford's University Avenue. Single-lighted candles glow and flicker in the windows of the antebellum homes that align the streets that are half-filled with people doing their last-minute Christmas shopping. Brightly colored Christmas lights are breaking into a mist of darkness that is about to settle in with the families that are gathering to celebrate the birth of Jesus Christ.

"How beautiful," Mary observes.

"Yeah," Joe agrees.

"I've seen no beauty in anything since Edward left me," Eleanor confesses and takes off her dark spectacles.

"I'm sorry to hear that," Mary says.

Joe acknowledges, "Me too. What about Layne? Don't you two have any fun together?"

Eleanor replaces his question with another, "Mary wrote to me that you were interested in writing. Tell me now, what kind of writing do you do?"

"Well, I am interested in writing. But to telling you what kind of writing I do, I'm not sure that I can," Joe says, scratching his head. "I just write."

"Joe wants to be a writer of sorts," Mary offers.

"Mary! For God's sake, you make me sound stupid!" Joe shouts.

Eleanor perks up, smoothes her dress, then asks, "Ohohohoh of sorts, eh?"

"All I do is teach English and Literature at the local high school during the week. I write on the weekends and in my spare time," Joe tells Eleanor.

"At the Vespers High School in Meridian," Mary offers.

Eleanor's face becomes illuminated. "My Edward was a professor you know. Why, he's the one who began the mosaic and writing in the memory books that Mordecai and William are trying to finish up," she says, pausing and gently stroking the diamond in the center of an antique diamond and amethyst ring set in a sterling silver scroll setting. "Yes, a wall mosaic is what I believe it's called." She turns to Joe, and asks matter-of-factly, "Would you like to see it?"

Mary throws a suspicious look Eleanor's way. Joe cries out, "You bet I would! What's it about?" His eyes widen. He increases his grip on the steering wheel to a tight squeeze.

Eleanor is proud of Joe's interest. She trembles in her seat and explains, "Edward started out rewriting William Shakespeare's' *King Lear* in memory books. Why, I'll never know. When I think back, I can remember that he said that he wished that he could be as understanding of *our boy* Layne as Lear was of *his girl* Cordelia. You know, sometimes I can't think as clear as I used to think though I believe that spending time in my Reading Room has helped me over the years, somehow." She pierces her bottom lip with her front teeth and gives a regretful look out the car window before lamenting, "If only Edward hadn't of died when he did. Well, maybe Layne ... I suppose I'll never *really* know what *could have been*, only *what is*." She sighs and continues with, "What Mordecai and William have done with it, I suppose you'll have to see for yourself. I suspect it's not easy to finish what someone else has begun." She stops talking, and then looks at Joe to see his reaction.

Mary is watching her aunt in earnest.

Joe is controlling his emotions; afraid she'll take back her offer if he gets too excited.

Eleanor continues her thoughts, "That is *if* you are interested in the wall mosaic." After a long pause, she asks, *"Are you?"*

Now unable to contain his excitement, Joe cries out, "Of course, I'm interested! Just tell me when I can see it!"

Excited by Joe's enthusiasm she says, "Wonderful! Right after supper then. That is, if it sits well with Mordecai. You'll have to get his permission too," she tells him, trembling and whispering, "Soon it will be my birthday. Soon it will be Christmas Day..."

Joe punches the gas pedal, bringing them to the Garfield Road sign. He turns onto Beacon Street then into Fable Court, and for the first time since early morning, everyone in the car is smiling.

A WALK-THROUGH OVAL FREE-STANDING CHRISTMAS WREATH with plywood backing, various greenery, clear lights, and a giant, red velvet ribbon woven throughout until it is united with a golden bow that serves as its topper meets everyone's eyes when Joe pulls the Pontiac into Fable Court.

Eleanor claps her hands when Joe says, "Hot damn, you sure know how to put on the dog, don't you?!"

Once out of the car, he offers her a hand up the front steps, but before she accepts, she puts on her dark spectacles.

Mary lingers, smiling and watching the only two people she has left in the world to love. While Joe guides Eleanor through the walk-through oval free-standing Christmas wreath, Mary glances at her watch and sees that it is 6:15 p.m. When she looks up, she sees the last ray of Southern light glimmering through a long vertical side window of her aunt's house. She walks over and leans on a Magnolia tree and thinks how amazing it is that they are even in Oxford for their first Christmas as man and wife. She turns her body around and settles her eyes on a decrepit front porch swing and wonders how long it has been since anyone has sat in it as the North wind begins to blow its cutting December breeze, causing the swing to move. The certain night and perhaps snow will soon fall on Oxford, Mississippi. And it will soon be Christmas Day. She sighs before she goes inside to dress for supper.

In the center of the dining room table sits a handsome silver centerpiece from seventeenth-century London which holds an arrangement of white winter-flowering heather and bloodtwig dogwood branches. Surrounding the arrangement is a pair of silver candlesticks glowing with beeswax candles. The air smells of home cooking and Scotch pine. The cherry wood table is set with Desert Rose China. Mordecai is placing presents like periods at the end of sentences beneath tinseled, metallic, chenille gold sticks and stems that spell out their names.

The menu includes homemade cornbread chicken and dressing, cranberry sauce, fresh cream corn, piping hot bread, butter pats shaped like yellow camellias, hot coffee, ice tea, and tap water. Lemon icebox pie with brown meringue and a vanilla crust, a classic Southern six-layer coconut cake, chocolate pecan fudge, and white pecan and rainbow fruity jelly divinity are the desert choices. There is no birthday cake. Julius Caesar's red caviar sits on a bronze, crescent moon plate.

Mordecai seats Eleanor, who is still wearing her dark spectacles, at the head of the table. She always wears them to eat her meals.

While Mordecai serves the meal, Joe watches him prepare an extra plate off to the side of the kitchen. Joe observes Mordecai's lack of emotion and takes a deep breath before saying to him, "Mordecai, Eleanor told me about your wall mosaic."

Mordecai looks puzzled but says nothing. He continues to prepare the extra plate.

Joe blurts out, "I hope you don't mind me taking an eyeshot at it?"

Eleanor takes off her dark spectacles.

Mordecai looks from Eleanor to Joe then down at the extra plate before asking, "I suppose that means you want to meet Layne. Do you?"

Eleanor looks stunned and Joe becomes excited while Mary looks suspiciously at Mordecai, trying to figure out why he's so cold and totally unreadable.

"Why, sure! I want to meet my cousin," Joe says with enthusiasm.

Eleanor trembles and smiles at Joe. She covers her mouth like she might burst with excitement. Her mood is lifted with Joe's enthusiasm.

"What I would like to know is *why* didn't Layne come and eat with us? Is he okay?" Mary asks.

Mary's questions upset Eleanor. She puts on her dark spectacles.

"Now, Babydoll, of course he's okay! Why, he's probably down with a cold or watching television," Joe offers, not wanting to upset Eleanor for fear she'll change her mind about him seeing the wall mosaic which might lead to him meeting Layne.

"Oh, I don't think Layne has a cold. Does he Mordecai?" Eleanor asks with concern.

Mordecai says, "No."

"Jesus Christ!" Joe mumbles under his breath.

"*You* may see him if Mordecai agrees," Eleanor tells Joe.

"What about me? He's my cousin too," Mary says, giving her aunt a hurtful look.

Eleanor ignores her and stands from the table, walking away from the dining room table and heading for another part of the house. She calls back, "Mary, come in here. I have a gift for you."

Mordecai turns and gives a soulful look to the Farmers. In turn, Joe offers him a smile. In response, Mordecai lets him know that he is willing to trust him when he says, "By the kind gods, 'tis well with thee, my new friend."

Joe winks at Mary. She gets up from the table and returns his wink. She notices the supper tray with the extra plate and its generous helpings of food on the kitchen countertop. She makes her way to the narrow hall, wondering why none of them opened their dinner presents.

"Marrr-y?" Eleanor calls out.

"I'll be right there! Wait another minute," she calls back to her aunt, entering their bedroom.

First, she checks her teeth in an antique box-shaped mahogany mirror that's hanging independently of a chest of drawers. Then she checks her pocket for the mint-flavored snuff. She reaches on top of a little round table and picks up a jade elephant with red ruby eyes, presses its tail with her thumb until a blue flame of fire appears from the end of its trunk. She laughs and replaces the lighter on the round table and brushes her pocket making contact with the glass of mint-flavored snuff before leaving the bedroom.

"All right, my dear," Eleanor calls back.

Back in the Franklin kitchen, Mordecai walks over to a side window, and when he reaches to pull back the drapes, he sees Newton Knight lurking outside burying the dead doe amid two tall Mississippi pines. He groans.

BELLADONNA, 1888—SOMEWHERE IN NEW ENGLAND

I N THE FRONT PARLOR, Eleanor is admiring the bare Christmas tree. After a short while, she walks over to a little table inside the narrow hallway, opens a drawer, then takes out an envelope. She gives it the once-over before putting it back inside the drawer. She walks over to another table and picks up a wrapped gift shaped like a shoe box. When Eleanor hears Mary's footsteps and her call out, "Here I come," she smiles.

Julius Caesar, whom they haven't seen since dinner, joins Mary in her walk. He is still wearing his neck watch and has a red stain around his mouth from the caviar, giving him the look of a bloodstained face. He walks alongside Mary. His initials snake down his back. She reaches down and lifts him into her arms. He frets a little, rejecting Mary's cleanup efforts when she dabs at the red stain with her hanky. "Julius Caesar, now I bet you know what's going on around here, don't you?" Mary understands his nodding head as agreement. He winks at her with his yellow eye.

"And to think of all the cold children running around Oxford without so much as an orange to put in their stocking for Christmas, not to mention a white fur coat like you got!" she scolds the Persian cat. His blue eye is frozen straight ahead. Julius Caesar smiles up at her. She places him on the floor. He runs ahead of her to find Eleanor. "Sweet Jesus, you look cuter than those Christmas puppies I saw this morning back in Increase, Mississippi!"

"Come on in here. I have a surprise for you," Eleanor tells her niece.

"What in the world?" Mary asks, walking into the parlor.

"Here, this is for you. Go on and open it before William gets here," she encourages Mary. She hands her a gift.

The gift is wrapped in tissue paper that has a delicate golden-vine background with scarlet grapes, purple plums, red cherries, yellow-green pears, and iridescent oranges, and various shades of antique greens amid peaches tipped with pearly white camellias alongside baby blue daisies, all of which look like they are growing amid a silent Garden of Eden.

Julius Caesar begins to strut around the parlor. When Mary gives him a quick glance, Eleanor tells her, "Don't mind him. He's as nosey as you can imagine."

Mary rips the tissue paper off the gift and marvels, "Oh, Aunt Eleanor, it's an old

Jerusalem Bible! Why, just holding it *moves* me to tears." She hugs her aunt. "I love old books. Thank you so much! I'll treasure it forever. I promise!"

Delight fills Eleanor and causes her to tremble with excitement. "I'm so glad you like it. It's a book that Joe can learn to love too. My dear, *it is you* that must teach him by example and nothing more."

"Uncle Edward's second love was for books, wasn't it?"

"It still is."

"Why, whatever do you mean?"

"Edward's love for books hasn't changed. Because he's in a long sleep that has outlasted our love doesn't mean he's changed what he loves. He never loved me. He never loved me. He *never* loved me or Layne either for that matter! Mary, it's the truth."

"Aunt Eleanor, what do you mean?"

"I feel guilty like it's my fault he left us early on in our lives. I did the best I knew how to do. I guess I never knew how to be married. I was just a child myself when we run away to Mississippi together. He was the ruler of me. Of everything. He always had to *rule over* me then us—Layne and me."

"You can't be serious?!"

"Indeed, I am serious. Charles Edward Franklin rules Fable Court even now—

from the grave."

"Aunt Eleanor, did Uncle Edward do something to hurt you or Layne? You can trust me. I won't tell if that's what you are worried about. I promise."

Without a moment's hesitation, "Day after day, Edward blamed me for his unhappiness. He said if I would have acted right that our life together would have been normal and that he never would have slapped my face or bullwhipped Layne. After he brought me to Mississippi, nothing I ever did was right. He swore I was born with bad genes and blamed it on Poppa's love for Scotch whiskey. He said Poppa passed his bad genes along to me and that was why he frequented the White House on campus and sought out boys for *Southern comfort*," she pauses then says soft and low, "and *unmentionables!*"

"Oh, my God! No! There's not one bit of truth in that! Aunt Eleanor, if it is true, how *could you* continue to love him after all *that*?"

"Even though Edward said that I was nothing without him and did *unmentionables* to others, his words and actions amid the Southern day or its night never changed my love for him."

"Why not?"

"You don't stop loving someone because of what they do or don't do to you. Genuine love never dies. Even death can't come between lovers. I know that better than anyone. I am tormented by my love for Edward. I love him. I hate him. I love him again. I hate him more. In the end, love always wins over hate—at least in my heart."

"Tell me, how *did* you come to marry Uncle Edward?"

"It was so long ago."

"Here, sit down and tell me. We've got a few minutes before Mr. Faulkner arrives. Besides, Joe can keep him entertained until we join them."

ELEANOR'S SPIRIT TAKES HER BODY AND MIND back in time to her childhood home, Belladonna, somewhere in New England where it is December 24, 1888.

"Merry Christmas!" Eleanor Beatrice Godwin says looking into an oval-shaped mirror with no frame while her mother looks on smiling.

"Honey Bea, you look perfect! I can't believe you will be sixteen tomorrow!" Adele Godwin says, tugging at her daughter's thin waistline.

"Momma, do you think I'm prettier than Belladonna at Christmastime?"

"Of course!"

Belladonna is a two-story Greek Revival house that has nestled itself between the ocean and a mountain-like bed of rocks south of a New England lighthouse for over one hundred years. The house has clipboard siding, a hipped roof, interior end chimneys, a front façade—five bays in width—a front door surrounded by narrow lights and a central pedimented portico supported by paired columns with Doric capitals that act like a shield between the ocean and Her people. An array of New England's aristocrats is gathering together for Eleanor's *Sweet Sixteen* birthday party. Eleanor smiles at herself in the mirror when Adele tells her, "Remember to keep your girlish figure for as long as you can." She teases her, "Don't drink anything but champagne tonight!"

Eleanor rolls her eyes before saying, "Yes, Momma." She gives Adele an anxious look and then checks herself in the mirror. "Do you think Edward Franklin will like my chatelaine braids fastened with Christmas roses?"

"I should think he would. Why you look lovely! I'm going to the Reading Room before he gets here. When you are finished primping, go join your Poppa and greet your guests," she says and gives her daughter a warm, loving smile. Both are wearing Vintage Victorian.

Eleanor shrugs her shoulders then giggles, pretending not to notice that Adele is leaving the room. She turns back to face the mirror before she says to her reflection, "I *hope* that Edward likes my hair." She checks her lips, rolls them together, and blows a little kiss into midair towards Adele's backside. Out of the corner of her eye, she catches a glimpse of a painting, *Lavacourt: Sunshine and Snow* by Claude Monet dated 1881. Beneath the painting is a pair of dark spectacles.

Adele walks towards an in-house elevator that has a little red door with a brass gate that must be released by the turn of a key. She stops in front of the elevator then reaches to punch a small, knobby black button before she inserts her key. She is tall, lean, and lovely. Once inside the elevator, Adele bounces like a breath of fresh air on the balls of her feet. When the elevator stops, she gets out on the second floor and goes to the Reading Room. She stops once again before reaching down to a glass-top cherry wood coffee table and picks up loose pages of what appears to be someone's writing. Adele reads aloud from the cover page, *The Happy Prince and Other Tales* by Oscar Wilde. She smiles.

She turns a loose page over and reads aloud, "'*Sweet Eleanor, may you always remember that Life has its own philosophy, but only you can find it for yourself. You should readily treat all the trivial things within yourself quite seriously and treat the serious things of Life with sincere and studied triviality. I pray that you always stay "bright and happy" and, more importantly, stay earnest. Happy early Birthday! Oscar Wilde December 1887.*'"

Adele turns, leaves the Reading Room, and takes the elevator to level one where she joins Eleanor and her father Nolan Godwin. Young well-dressed suitors wait their turn in a line to the left of a five-foot high German chocolate birthday cake. There is an ice carving of the number sixteen sitting in the middle of a fountain that is overflowing with champagne. Guests take turns holding their glasses beneath the steady stream of the gold, bubbly brew.

Eleanor gives Nolan a shy look and then smiles before saying, "Oh, my, Poppa, would you look at all those boys in their finest? Who shall I dance with first?"

Nolan gives a long, proud look around the room that is ringing with music before he shouts, "They had better stand in line for my little girl!" He pauses before asking, "Are you happy?"

They begin to dance to *Plaisir d'amour*—the pleasure of love.

Eleanor looks around before answering with, "Oh, Poppa, please! I'm not a little girl anymore!" She takes a deep breath and strokes her lips with her pointer finger. "Oh, yes, I'm very happy." Both smile when Adele waves over to them. They stop dancing, and Nolan bows to Eleanor before they both turn and walk out of Belladonna. As they stand in the center of the front porch, the lighthouse is giving off a shadow, causing them to look like two figures frozen deep within a snow globe. A full moon casts its lapis glow over the ocean's waves from a pitch-black sky. Nolan reaches into his front vest pocket and brings out a little round gold pillbox and takes a dip of snuff from it. He offers it to Eleanor who takes her own pinch of snuff.

"Is this snuff flavored with mint leaves? It's good," Eleanor asks Nolan.

"Yes, it's flavored with mint. I got it on my last trip to Newport, Rhode Island. Got a lad to grind the mint leaves fresh just for you. Paid him a nickel. Don't tell your mother either."

"*I'll never tell her anything,*" Eleanor thinks.

Nolan looks over at the lighthouse and says, "Eleanor, did you know that there's a great magic lens at the top of the lighthouse that, when I was a boy, could focus its light and set enemy ships ablaze?"

"Oh, Poppa, don't you grow tired of telling me that story?"

"Never," he tells her, darting his eyes up at the lens of the lighthouse.

"Let's go back inside. I want to see if Edward Franklin has arrived."

"Eleanor, please stay away from that Southerner! What could *he* possibly give you? Has he even finished his education? What's he going into? Medicine? Politics?" he asks.

"Poppa, Edward is a good man! He's kind. Smart too. He's going to be a professor at the University of Mississippi."

"A professor? What kind of money would he make? I tell you what, you and that mother of yours. What kind of a professor? How old a man is he? What kind of a family does he come from?"

"Poppa! Why do you have to put a price on everything? I tell you, Edward's a good catch. He's going to teach Shakespeare and Latin. He's thirty."

Nolan spits out his snuff, then shouts out, "Thirty is too old for you!" He considers then asks, "Shakespeare and Latin, eh?"

She smiles at him, and then announces, "Poppa, I want to marry him. Please, don't get angry. I love Edward. He's a good man like you."

"Nonsense! Why, you don't even know him. Does your mother know what you're up to? Or is this *her* idea!" He considers once again. "Love, eh? Like me, eh? He *is* a good-looking man. But, for God's sake, marriage?"

"Don't lose your temper, Poppa, Edward reads poetry to me."

Nolan looks up at the full moon before he points over towards Belladonna and says, "Reads poetry to you. Hell, Eleanor, you will never have anything if you go down to Mississippi and marry a damn

Southerner. Never! Listen to me; there are at least a dozen or so *fine young* men in there that would give you a place in New England or even in New York Society. Don't jump and ruin your life because somebody *reads* to you."

He mumbles to himself, "*Damn it to hell!*"

Eleanor spits her snuff out, takes her Poppa by the arm, and pulls him towards the door before he can say another word. Once the guests see them entering Belladonna, they begin to sing *Happy Birthday, Honey Bea*. The room goes dark, and balloons fall from the ceiling leaving only the light from the lighthouse showing faint images of the Godwins and their guests dancing like ghosts from another time.

When the lights come back on, Edward Franklin is standing in front of Eleanor. Although Edward is quite a handsome man, his body movements—his walk, his hand gestures—resemble a woman. He bows and says with a lulling Southern accent, "Happy Birthday, *Honey Bea*! Pray I have the next dance?"

She laughs, and then says, "Yes, my Lord."

They dance across the length of the room to the music while everyone looks on with anticipation. Nolan takes Adele by the hand and they dance. Eleanor's other prospective suitors stand in a complete circle around the two handsome couples like characters in a Shakespearean play.

"Edward, I told Poppa that I love you," Eleanor tells Edward. He whirls her around the room. She takes a deep breath before asking, "When are you going to ask him for my hand?"

Edward smiles with approval. "Did you now?" He waits a minute before in a controlling tone he adds, "So, you're *imposing* yourself on me already, are you?"

"I don't know what you mean."

"Let me be the man and you be the woman," he tells her, raising his eyebrows. "Now is a good time to speak to Nolan."

She rolls her eyes and gives him a doubtful look.

"What has he said about us?" he asks her.

"Poppa wants me to be happy. He loves me *the most*, don't you know?"

"Have you told him that you're going back to Mississippi with me?"

"I told him that I wanted to marry you."

He cups his chin and looks around the room. "I'll *tell* him then. Listen, Eleanor, I learned a long time ago that when you want something that sometimes you have to be forceful and show people who are giving you, well, an opposition of sorts, the way it's going to be whether they like it or not."

No answer.

"Well, answer me, damn it!"

"I tried to tell him the best way I knew how. He seems to be in a good mood for you to talk to him about it now though."

Edward seems pleased. He gives her a kiss on the cheek, escorts her to a chair, and then walks over to her parents. Nolan has spotted him and nudges Adele to look in his direction. Adele flashes the young Mississippian a bright smile. She is stunning for her age. Nolan becomes more agitated when he sees Edward walking towards them like he knows what's about to happen.

"Adele, I won't have *my* daughter marry a damn Southerner! I don't care what kind of an education he has. I can't have it! What will people say? They will laugh at us for eternity!"

"Nolan, please don't make a scene! Not tonight on Bea's birthday," Adele tells him. Edward joins them. Instead of Nolan greeting Edward, he storms out of the room.

Nolan's burst of rudeness provokes Edward to turn to Adele and shaking his fist he declares, "I will marry Eleanor with or without his blessing!"

Adele is caught in the middle facing Edward. She tries to give him a genuine smile but can't. The music plays louder. Eleanor runs out the front door after Nolan. Edward turns to follow, but Adele grabs him by the arm and says, "Let them be alone. Please let them go. You can talk to Nolan another time." She takes a deep breath before she says in a pleading tone, "Let them be, please. It's our daughter's birthday—please don't make a scene."

Edward does not reply. He gives Adele an angry look and pulls a small round green velvet box from his front pocket, opens it, and shows her a diamond and amethyst ring in a sterling silver scroll setting.

Adele blinks twice but says nothing.

Nolan and Eleanor stand on the south side of Belladonna in the roving light of the lighthouse while the waves of the ocean splash recklessly on the rocks. Neither speak as blue, orange, aqua, and clear Christmas lights blink amid a a dark fog. They begin to argue. The magic of the lighthouse begins to focus a bright light on them, causing them to look like they may be set ablaze any minute.

ELEANOR GODWIN AND EDWARD FRANKLIN are sitting on a train arm in arm. He looks happy. She looks depressed. Neither is talking. Silently, they sit looking out a window while a teenage boy wearing a cowboy hat sitting in front of them begins to strum on a guitar and sing, *"You, you on the road / Ah yes, you must have a reason to love / Don't ever ask the Lord why 'cause if you knew the answer you* would cry / *Just look ahead before you die and know that I lo-ah-ve you!*"

A sign flashes past their window that reads, *Atlanta, Georgia, 30 miles.*

Behind the newlyweds, an older woman is trying to comfort the cry of an ear-piercing newborn. Eleanor turns around in her seat to offer help and asks, "Do you want me to take him?"

The woman checks her wristwatch and then shakes her head before saying, "No. Thank you for offering though, but no. You see, well, both his parents were killed instantly in an automobile accident last night."

Eleanor gasps.

The teenage boy stops playing his guitar to listen.

Edward continues to stare out the train window, unmoved.

"You see, I'm just the nurse in charge of transporting him to Goodlife, Mississippi, where his mother's sister lives," she tells them. "And, of course, his parents."

The teenage boy sits up straighter and cocks his head their way when Eleanor asks, "*His parents?*"

"Yes. Both caskets are on the train. I saw that they were put on myself. In car Number 37. They were Russells. I won't take the responsibility if something happens to their corpses. Know what I mean?" she asks Eleanor, who doesn't answer her because both her eyes are frozen straight on Edward who still hasn't given the ear-piercing cry of the baby a second thought, never mind the first glance while he twists at a tight gold band on his left ring finger.

Eleanor sighs and covers her ears.

"AUNT ELEANOR, are you okay?" Mary asks, more concerned about her aunt after observing her go into another state of mind without speaking a single word. Without warning, a playful Julius Caesar hurls himself into the Christmas tree and startles them.

"Belladonna," she says to Mary, still in a dazed state of mind until they hear echoes of "Tap tap tap, tap tap tap," from the brass door knocker of Fable Court.

Mary places a hand on her aunt's shoulder and asks, "You married Uncle Edward at Belladonna?"

"No. Somewhere in New England. I fell in love at Belladonna though. You know, he never read any more poetry to me after we were married. I never understood what came over him from time to time. He was never predictable. He was dark inside. It was like he was two different people." She signs. "The Southern light in Mississippi was beautiful from day one. It helped lift my spirits but never his. Charles Edward Franklin was always in the dark. Still, I hate that I love him."

Mary gives her a curious look.

"That must be William Faulkner. I'll go let him in. You go see if you can fetch Joe away from Mordecai," Eleanor tells Mary. Her mind has returned her back to Oxford.

While Mary gives her aunt a hug, she says, "Only if you will promise me that we will continue our conversation later."

"I'd like that very much. Yes, I'd like that very much," Eleanor says and heads towards the front door. Mary places the Jerusalem Bible in the center of a glass-top cherry coffee table that is divided by a mint-colored Depression glass. Julius Caesar jumps onto the coffee table and makes himself comfortable next to it. Eleanor is wearing her dark spectacles.

"I'VE NEVER SEEN a mosaic before," Joe says to Mordecai standing in front of the wall mosaic.

The mosaic has dusty brown, light yellow, opaque pearly white, soft bronze and gold with hints of scarlet red tiles arranged in the shape of fives loaves of bread and two fishes amid a sand-like and somewhat opaque background that's surrounded with patch-like squares of azure Venetian glass that have been shaped into a lake that is draining into a river. A bluff overlooks a sea. Joe observes a glass of water along with an open bottle of Port wine and a loaf of pumpernickel bread sitting nearby.

"Byzantine?" Joe asks.

Mordecai nods.

Although Mordecai is holding the supper tray, he frees a hand and points to an area on the right side of the mosaic that is made of pottery and chunks of dark wood that form the silhouettes of twelve fishermen and says to Joe, "Pieces of the streets of Oxford and hunks of William's old barn. He and Layne gather them when they go out. William has been good to take Layne out for years treating him like his own son. Only William had the temerity to call on Fable Court. Most of Oxford fell out with the Franklins years ago. No one can remember why."

Joe is standing back from the wall when he asks, "Mordechai, did you do this entire mosaic yourself?"

"No. Edward began it many years ago. It was William who took apart what he'd done so Layne could learn a skill. Like a trade, I guess. I work on it, as best I can. William has tried his hand at it for years, though he likes to write in the memory books Edward left behind. It was Layne who chose the fish," Mordecai replies, pointing to the memory books.

"My, God! Mordecai, what I'm seeing here breaks all the rules of nature—it's the story of *The Loaves and Fishes—the Power and Presence*. A great miracle of the Bible where Jesus Christ feeds 5000 people with five loaves of bread and two fishes by looking up into heaven and blessing them. This is *priceless*," Joe marvels.

Mordecai shrugs and with eyes wide open investigates the supper tray.

When Joe reaches for a memory book and begins reading aloud from it, Mordecai hears voices in his head.

Joe reads, "*Has his sons brought him to Oxford? Wouldst thou give thy sons all?*" Joe pauses and looks to Mordecai for an explanation, but Mordecai only raises his eyebrows at him, looking away while the voices ring even clearer in his imagination.

Fool: He hath no sons, sir. Just one.

Lear: Death, traitor! Nothing could have subdued nature To such a lowness but his unkind son. It is the fashion, that discarded fathers Should have thus little mercy on his flesh? Judicious punishment! 'twas this flesh that begot That pelican son."

Joe stops reading, looks down on the memory book page, and takes in a deep breath before saying, "Mordecai, what's *Eleanor* got to do with this?"

Mordecai still does not answer; instead, he walks over to a long, vertical side window and looks out at the new moon. A deep sadness enters his face.

"*Eleanor,*" Joe reads, "*Pillicock sat on Pillicock Hill. No. Alow, alow, loo, loo!*"

Mary enters the room.

"*William,*" Joe reads and adds, "*This cold night will turn us all to fools and madmen.*" He pauses for a minute and looks at Mary.

Mary frowns but doesn't speak. She sees a reddish plant with bell-shaped flowers and shining black berries sitting in the darkest corner of the room. She forgets to tell them that someone is at the front door. She looks into the wall mosaic, then at Joe, "This is beautiful! What does it mean? Where's Layne?"

Joe does not reply. Instead, he continues reading,

"*Edward: No words, no words! Hush.*"

"*William: He that endureth to the end shall be saved!*"

The Oxford voices stop in Mordecai's imagination when a new voice speaks from behind the wall. Mary's eyes widen. Joe looks to Mordecai when it asks, "Mordecai, is that you? Did you bring me any cheese? I'm so lonely. It's dark in here. My bird wants seeds. He is hungry too."

Mordecai looks more alert and takes a firmer hold of the supper tray, walks over to the far right corner of the mosaic to the patch-like squares of azure Venetian glass that have been shaped into the lake that is draining into a river, bends down and looks into two peep holes.

Mary follows and asks, "Layne, is that you? Layne?"

"No words, no words. Hush," Mordecai tells Mary.

Mordecai's words make Joe mad. He walks over and yells, "Mordecai, don't talk to my wife like that! What's going on here? Open up this wall!" He leaves the memory book behind.

Mordecai isn't alarmed by Joe; instead, he looks relieved and hands the supper tray to Mary. When he knocks three times above the two peep holes, the hidden door of the wall mosaic opens.

SOMEONE MUST HAVE PLUGGED IN the walk-through oval free-standing Christmas wreath because when William Faulkner arrives it is all aglow. Eleanor doesn't know this, so she stops to check and see if it's plugged in. She unplugs it, and then plugs it in again causing its light to flicker. This startles William Faulkner enough that he stops tapping the brass door knocker, turns, and goes back through the oval Christmas wreath while laughing aloud. He staggers once again through the lighted oval, and when Eleanor opens the front door of Fable Court and their eyes meet, he shouts, "God save the King!"

Eleanor trembles, smiles but says nothing.

"Hello, Belladonna!" Faulkner blurts out, tracing Eleanor's smile without touching her face.

"Greetings and Merry Christmas Eve to you my good neighbor and friend," Eleanor says to Faulkner, taking off her dark spectacles and trying to collect her thoughts before saying, "Jesus is the reason for the season."

"Jesus is the reason for everything!" Faulkner shouts. Eleanor moves aside making room for his entrance. He isn't even inside when he asks, "Miss Eleanor, where do you keep your Scotch whiskey?"

"Now, William, before you start up with *that*, I want you to meet my niece Mary and her husband Joe," Eleanor tells him, looking towards the back of the house and not knowing that Mordecai is opening the door hidden in the wall mosaic with Joe and Mary looking on.

"Layne, come out," Mordecai says to the wall mosaic.

Even though he's beyond middle age, Mary and Joe see that a manchild has joined them. At first, the manchild looks startled to see them, and then, his face takes on a friendly look. He smiles. He's dressed in a long-sleeved red checkerboard cotton shirt with navy-blue pants. Startlingly to them, he is wearing a black leather patch over his right eye.

He looks from Mary to Joe and asks, "Who you?"

Mary looks at Joe who looks at Mordecai, but no one says anything. Layne walks over to Mary and sets his eyes on the tray of food. Mordecai's face becomes intense. His eyes follow Layne's every move. It's obvious to the Farmers that Mordecai feels much love towards him.

"Mordecai?" Layne asks, eyeing his guests.

Mordecai approaches Mary and takes the tray from her. Mordecai seats Layne on the floor where he begins to eat with his hands like a starved animal. First, he goes for the cream corn and shoves it into his mouth with the fistfuls. Cranberry sauce is his next choice. He takes it between his forefingers and puts it on his thumb. In one breath, he sucks it down his throat without even chewing. He cups the chicken and dressing with his hand and tries to fit the entire serving into his mouth.

Joe gasps.

"He's eating his Christmas Eve dinner like a wild animal!" Mary wails, then lowers her voice to a whisper. "Mordecai, he looks fine to me though. I thought that there was something terribly wrong with him." She stops talking and turns to Joe to ask, "Joe, how does he look to you?"

"He looks fine to me except for the black leather eye patch." He turns to Mordecai and asks him, "Why is he wearing an eye patch?" Mordecai ignores Joe's question.

"Mordecai, aren't you going to introduce him to us?" Mary asks.

Mordecai looks relieved when he points to them and says, "Layne, these are your cousins, Mary and Joe Farmer."

Layne ignores Mordecai. His face lights up when he goes for the brown meringue on the lemon icebox pie with his left hand.

Joe walks over to the wall and asks, "How long has he been like this? Or in there?"

Mary is watching Layne eat.

"Ever since Edward died, save for when William takes him out to walk the land with his Jack Russell Terriers," Mordecai replies.

Layne looks up like he knows what Mordecai has told Joe. Although he looks like a clown with the brown meringue around his mouth, he still manages to look scared. He darts his left eye at everyone. Mordecai is quick to give him a nod of assurance, and then he goes back to eating his dinner.

"Why, Uncle Edward has been dead at least twenty years or more, hasn't he? Layne couldn't have possible been in there for *that* long, could he?"

Mordecai answers, "That's what Eleanor ordered until one of us finishes the wall mosaic or William or I fill the memory books. Neither one of us have been able to finish something which we didn't start, though we never run out of words to write in the memory books. William says that real art like a good book—can never be finished by anyone. That's why I'm glad you two accepted Eleanor's invitation. Now maybe we can get Layne out of here!" Mordecai gives the Farmers a hopeful look.

"I've never heard of such an awful thing in all my born days," Joe cries out. He assesses Layne before telling Mordecai, "He looks so good. You've taken good care of him, haven't you?" He pauses, collects his thoughts. "Can he talk much? Why does he have that eye patch on?"

Mary is watching Layne's every move. After he finishes his dinner, he begins to take more notice of her and Joe. Mordecai walks over and wipes him off with a wet dishrag he had hidden under the dinner plate. A look of exhaustion appears across Mordecai's face when he tells them, "Only God knows how hard I've tried to take care of him."

He takes a deep breath and says, "He lost his right eye—." He pauses to collect his thoughts and places a hand on Layne's shoulder, smiling at his longtime friend. "Layne, they are your family. It's okay. Tell them hello."

Joe interrupts with, "What do you mean, he lost his right eye?"

"He lost it before I came here. That's all I know to tell you. Every December, it bleeds," Mordecai tells them while Layne looks on.

Mary looks horrified. Joe throws Mordecai an appalled look.

Layne gives Mary a suspicious look. He walks up to Joe and asks again, "Who you?"

Mary is touched by his innocence and reaches out and offers him her hand.

"I'm your cousin, Joe. Joe Farmer. Can you say my name?"

Layne smiles and says, "Joe," and takes Mary's hand and says, "Momma?"

"Lord, no! I'm your cousin too, Mary. Mary Farmer. Your momma and my momma are sisters," she tells him and begins to talk much louder than normal, "Can you say, Mary?"

"Mary, he's not deaf," Joe comments.

Layne says, "Guitar."

She waits, as if hoping for more, but he says nothing else; instead he turns around and runs back into the wall mosaic. She shrugs. "What does he mean by saying *guitar?*" Mary asks Mordecai. Joe scratches his head.

"Oh, he's got a guitar in there. He wants you to see it. Wait just a minute and see if he comes out with it," Mordecai replies.

"Ah," she says.

When Layne runs back into the room holding up a guitar, Joe winks at Mary.

"Mordecai give me this guitar! See?" he tells them.

Mordecai smiles.

"Oh, it's so nice! Can you play it?" Mary asks and returns Joe's wink.

"Would you look at that guitar?" Joe comments, looking impressed.

"You pretty!" Layne tells Mary.

Again, she asks him with an even louder voice, "I said, can you play it?"

"Mary, the boy is not deaf," Joe tells her again.

"Who said he was?" Mary asks, actually wondering what Joe meant.

"Oh, just forget it!"

Layne begins shaking his head with excitement while smiling from ear to ear. He shouts out, "Elvis play it!"

Mordecai gives Layne a fatherly smile.

Layne gazes from Mary to Joe until he hears Eleanor call out, "Mary, Joe, our company has arrived!"

Layne looks at Mordecai and asks, "Momma?"

"Yes, that's your Momma calling out. But you *know how she is*," Mordecai tells him and hangs his head.

Layne nods, flashing a smile before saying, "Julius?"

Mary interrupts with, "Mordecai, what do you mean, he *knows how she is?*"

Mordecai looks rushed, so much that Joe senses that they need to stop with their questions, so he says, "Mary, I think there's a lot more to this than Mordecai has time to tell us, right?"

Mordecai nods.

Layne walks over to Joe and points to the cigarettes in his shirt pocket and shouts, "You stink!" He makes an ugly face at Joe, leading to a loud burp. "Excuse me!"

"I probably do stink from my smokes! I'll have to quit them while I'm here," Joe says, winking at Mary. "I'm glad we came too, but I want you to know that this whole *mosaic wall business* sounds pretty ridiculous to me. Besides, I don't know if anyone's Shakespeare is *that* good to even understand it all much less write in one of those *strange* memory books!"

Everyone laughs.

Once again, "Momma?" Layne asks of Mary.

"Layne! Don't be rude!" Mordecai scolds him and explains to Mary, "He thinks all women are called mommas."

Mary turns and smiles at Mordecai. He doesn't return her smile. Instead, he turns towards the wall mosaic and says in a sad voice, "Yes Joe, there's a lot more. I'm glad somebody came. I didn't know what else to do." He closes his eyes and drifts off into another time before he opens them and confesses, "I can't seem to finish anything anyone else started—the wall mosaic mainly, nor can I get Eleanor to let the boy live like he should." He gives them another hopeful look before saying, "Now that you two are here, maybe you can do something with her." He turns and stares deep at the wall and then back at Joe before asking, "Or maybe *you can* finish up the wall mosaic so the madness will stop? I'm tired of taking her confusing orders. William is the only one who is willing to put up with her foolishness. Or madness."

Layne looks around the room and asks, "Where's Billy? He and his Jacks here for me?"

Joe looks at Layne and asks, "Can he come with us now, or will it upset Eleanor if we take him out into the parlor without asking her first?"

"No, no, no. She couldn't take seeing him! You two go on out and I'll be right along after I get him ready for bed," Mordecai says while wringing his hands.

Mary looks at the wall and wails, "Joe, we can't leave him alone on Christmas Eve. Not in his own house!"

Layne likes Mary's tone of voice and gives her a hopeful look.

Joe says, "Babydoll, we have to respect Mordecai's wishes. After all, he's been around here a lot longer than we have, and Layne seems to be fine. We've got to figure out a way to get him out of here, but if we make your aunt mad at Mordecai, there's no telling what she might do."

Joe turns to Layne and asks, "You okay, Layne?"

Mordecai sighs.

Layne cocks his head in question at Joe but says nothing.

Joe asks again, "You okay, Layne?"

"I okay. Come to see my bird?" he asks Joe.

Joe takes Mary's hand and leads her over to where Layne is standing with his guitar.

"What?!" Mary yells out, startling Layne who sticks his fingers in his ears and eyes her suspiciously.

Joe gives him a wink and clucks his tongue once murmuring, "*Women.*"

Layne smiles. Mordecai takes him by the hand and guides him back into the wall mosaic. Layne flings back the words, "No words, no words! Hush!"

The Farmers walk over, look inside the peep holes, and watch as Mordecai lowers his eyes down at a floor that is made entirely of red Verona Italian marble while reaching to close a once high fashion scalloped and tasseled window shade on a vertical window.

MORDECAI IS SURPRISED when he returns from behind the wall and sees his new friends waiting for him. He asks, "Would you like to see *my* piece?"

"Of course, we would," Joe replies, and Mary nods.

Mordecai takes them into another room that is two doors deeper into the narrow hallway. As they walk, no one speaks. He reaches into his vest pocket and pulls out an antique little key with a floral motif at its head. He places it into a little hole above a brass doorknob, turns it, and swings the door open.

"What in the world?" Mary asks in a marveling voice.

"My room," Mordecai turns and tells her with Joe watching his every move. They walk across a Persian carpet while Mordecai flicks at a light switch. When the light comes on, they see a mural that covers all four walls of the room.

"Oh, my," Mary says, eyeing the piece.

"What's it called?"

No answer.

On the north wall of the room there is a peacock-blue sky and dark images in spirals resembling coils of blue-black smoke. No grass, no trees, no animals, no sun, no moon, no stars. No light. No life.

On the east wall is a man in early adulthood screaming with his head thrown back and his mouth open. His face is grief-stricken. He looks like Mordecai except older. He is standing beside an oven that is painted jet-black. A ribbon flanks his right side. The ribbon resembles a path and at its end is a red rose that leads to the west wall. Each petal of the rose has been precisely painted and is perfect in its three-dimensional structure. Pristine. Mary can't help herself and reaches to touch the red rose. Mordecai lifts his eyebrows when she jerks her hand back, realizing that it's not real. The petals are highlighted in a deeper scarlet color between a cinnamon and a burnt, fiery orange—like a mixture of anger and fear. Or blood. On the coppery stem of the rose are flecks of gold dotting a line of thorns. Above the old man are faces of people of all ages bearing a resemblance to one another like members of a family. The faces look devoid from life and love. Dead even.

"My God," Mary whispers.

Joe presses his fingers into her ribs, signaling her to be quiet.

Mordecai watches them for their reaction.

"Buchenwald," Joe reads the only word painted in fiery red and outlined in pitch-black on the east wall of the mural.

Mary asks Mordecai, "What does it all mean?"

He answers her with two words, "Death Camp."

The Farmers gasp.

"*Father?*" Mordecai mumbles.

"What did you say?" Joe asks him.

"I said, 'Father.' I mean, this is my father," he tells them adding, "*Was* my father."

Silence.

"Many voices came back to me after I came to Fable Court," Mordecai tells them. "Serving most of my life as a gravedigger before coming to Fable Court, I believe that I was cut off from my true destiny. My father and his body burning in the furnace hit me so hard as a small boy that I thought I'd never stand again. Even though I put it out of my mind for years, it all came back to me in Oxford. I seem to remember that when I was a small boy, I became a gravedigger to take suspicion off me. To save my own life. It kept me out of the furnaces."

"Mordecai, you don't have to tell us anything," Joe interrupts him.

"That's right," Mary agrees.

"I said, I believe that I was cut off from my true destiny. Best I can figure out in my own mind. For years, I've tried to put it all together by painting, but it's been like trying to paint hell. Hell, for the living, that is. I believe there is some reason I was left here and didn't die like the others—to take care the boy, maybe? I've always felt that I am responsible for ending something." He sighs.

Mary's eyes well up with tears. She pierces her bottom lip with her eye teeth.

"I am never satisfied with my piece. I don't think I can capture my own family's story."

"Oh, God!" Mary wails, moving Joe to put his arm around her. She asks, "How old are you or were you? Why, you must have been a very young boy when your father died."

"I'm not sure. I've never wanted to feel the pain that comes with knowing my age." Mordecai tells her. He pauses. "It doesn't matter because I matter to no one." He shrugs.

"Has painting helped you any?" Joe asks him.

Mary's eyes widen.

"Feel alive. Yes, my piece has helped me feel alive, especially when I work on it all night in the darkness of Fable Court. That is, it did help me *until* Eleanor started going to visit Edward in the cemetery. After I stay up all night painting, the next day I feel younger." he tells them.

Joe nods.

"What about your momma?" Mary asks.

"I don't remember her at all. For years I've tried to remember her name. I can't recall it at all," he says. He swallows hard. His face takes on the same grief-stricken look of the man near the oven. His cheeks sink in. His skin becomes parched. Thirsty. Joe and Mary to reach out their hands to offer him comfort.

It is apparent that Mordecai doesn't want their touch or their sympathy when he turns his back on them. He positions his body in front of his mural. Then with tears streaming down his face, he begins to trace the red rose one petal at a time. He goes on to trace the thorns of gold until the Farmers turn and walk out of the room without ever seeing the south wall.

WILLIAM FAULKNER'S DANCE

Chapter 10

THE FARMERS SEE William Faulkner and Eleanor sitting side by side on the settee talking when they enter the parlor of Fable Court.

"Where's Estelle?" Eleanor asks William Faulkner.

"Eleanor, she won't go anywhere with me after dark is all I can tell you," Faulkner tells her, shrugging his shoulders.

"Do tell," Eleanor says in amazement.

He nods.

"William, is she afraid of your driving or what?"

Standing, "Hell no! Eleanor, we can walk over here you know. If you want to know the truth about it, she's not *sociable* like I am," he tells her, taking off his houndstooth tweed duster. He rolls it up into a little ball before placing it in the corner of the settee.

Eleanor accepts what Faulkner tells her, but she has a regretful look on her face. "I see. It's no wonder you always look so lonely when you and your Jacks are walking by Fable Court."

He nods and tells her, "I've always been a lonely man."

When Eleanor looks and sees Mary and Joe standing off to the side of the parlor, she says, "Here are the children now."

William Faulkner jumps around, extends a wide-eyed Joe his left hand, and declares, "Merry Christmas to you, my boy!"

They shake. Then Faulkner reaches and kisses Mary's hand. She blushes and says, "Mister Faulkner, why are we mighty blessed to spend this Christmas Eve with you and Aunt Eleanor."

"Mr. Good God Almighty!" Joe begins before clearing his throat and clarifying his greeting. "I mean, Mr. William Faulkner! I can't believe that it's you!"

Faulkner sits down beside Eleanor who realizes that she hasn't properly introduced everyone, so she stands and says, "William, I want you to meet my niece, Mary, and her husband, Joe Farmer." She gives William a quick glance. and then she says, "Mary and Joe, this is my good neighbor and dear friend of many, many, many years, William Faulkner."

Once again everyone shakes hands.

Mordecai joins them.

"May I offer anyone some refreshment?" Mary asks.

"I like this boy!" Faulkner says of Joe and walks over and pats him on the back before he turns to face Mary and says, "But, you my dear are talking *real* Southern hospitality!"

Mary giggles and says, "I smell tobacco."

"William is partial to his pipe," Eleanor comments.

Faulkner looks over at the Christmas tree and asks, "Eleanor, where in Sam Hill did you find such a big tree?"

Mordecai leaves the parlor.

"I had it sent over from Ole Miss. Do you like it?" she asks him.

"Sure, I like it. Who wouldn't?" He stops talking and collects his thoughts before he says, "Goddamn, Eleanor, how do you plan to decorate it?"

Eleanor smiles sheepishly. Mordecai rolls in a refreshment cart. Mary gives her pocket a pat to check on the snuff and realizes that the piece of wood is still in her pocket too.

Faulkner rolls his eyes around the parlor without saying a word.

Eleanor glances over towards the Christmas tree and offers, "William, why I thought that we could all decorate it together and that maybe we could tell stories." She waits, but he doesn't respond. So, she presses, "Do you know any *new* stories? Are you working on a new book?"

Again, he looks around the parlor before he says, "Sounds right fine to me! Just point me and a bottle of Scotch in the right direction!" He cocks his head to the left side of the room before he adds, "I'm *always* working on a new book. You know that. But Eleanor, do you know a new or even an old tale to tell the children?"

Eleanor throws Faulkner a sincere smile. The Farmers see that she and Faulkner are on the same wavelength. Joe realizes that having them in the same room together feels electric. He shakes his hands feeling a surge of electricity. Mary looks at him like he's crazy, while a quiet, relieved Mordecai stands good-naturedly, by the refreshment cart waiting and willing to ever serve.

Mordecai speaks first, "Five minutes ago I saw a Confederate soldier burying a lifeless deer outside one of the side windows of Fable Court."

Eleanor rolls her neck around in Mordecai's direction.

Mary gives Joe a look that would crack a mirror.

When Mordecai sees everyone's reaction to what he has said, he looks at Eleanor for support. She comes to his defense. "Well, I believe that you saw a stranger with an animal in his care—be it or him—dead or alive."

Nodding, "Both were dead," Mordecai confirms.

Faulkner says, "Now, you two, I'm the storyteller around these parts, and if you aren't careful with your words, both of you will end up over at Whitfield like I do every so often to dry my bad self out!" He chuckles to himself. "Mississippi's finest asylum for all the sweet sons-of-bitches like me to congregate in every once in a while!"

Julius Caesar walks into the parlor and jumps up on top of the Jerusalem Bible, gazing over towards William Faulkner, stressed by the conversation—or by the man himself—and snarls.

Faulkner rubs his eyes before saying, "Eleanor, what in the holy hell has that goddamn Persian cat got on tonight?" He stops speaking and takes a second look at Julius Caesar and mumbles, "Go back to Rome, would you?"

Mary smiles at Joe.

Mordecai clears his throat.

The cat ignores him.

He says, "Eleanor, he has on a white fur coat—monogrammed no less—with a wristwatch strapped around his goddamn scrawny little neck." Faulkner looks up at the ceiling and sees an oatmeal lid string hanging in midair. He frowns then asks Eleanor, "Jesus Christ, what in the world is that goddamn oatmeal lid string doing up there?"

"That's to remind me to put a new light bulb in," Eleanor tells him.

Faulkner laughs, claps his hands, and says, "Well, that makes perfect sense to me!"

Eleanor smiles and nods at everyone.

Mary blushes.

Mordecai throws Joe an impatient look. Luckily, William understands the silent communication and says, "Everybody, how about Mordecai fixing us something to drink to get us in the Christmas spirit so that we can start decorating this big tree?"

Mordecai sighs.

Faulkner turns towards Eleanor and teases, "I hope that you know I can't stay here until next year!"

"William, you can come back for New Year's Eve *only if* I'm still here," Eleanor whispers.

Joe heads for the refreshment cart, but Mary turns to Faulkner encouraging him to tell a story. "Would you like to begin?" She stops speaking and turns to her aunt's direction. "Aunt Eleanor, can Layne come out and listen too?"

Eleanor reaches into her front dress pocket and draws out her dark spectacles.

Faulkner gives her an astonished look. "Since when do you let the boy out?"

Eleanor puts on her dark spectacles.

Mary looks around the parlor while pleating at her bottom lip with her fingers and repeats herself, "Aunt Eleanor, can Layne come out and listen too?"

Faulkner turns and faces Eleanor and asks, "Eleanor, what in the holy hell has happened to your eyes?" She looks straight ahead. He rolls his eyes around the parlor. "Where is that boy of yours? Hell, for once, let him out, won't you?"

She ignores his last question but answers his first with, "Oh William, my eyes are about to quit on me."

Faulkner appears shocked, wheels around again, and then blurts out, "Good God Almighty! When did this happen?"

Julius Caesar, who is sitting on the Jerusalem Bible, begins to purr when Eleanor removes her dark spectacles and shows everyone her eyes. "They look better than they are." She folds then places her dark spectacles in her front pocket.

Faulkner settles back into the settee. "The *Good Book* says that the lamp of the body is the eye." He gives Eleanor a wise look. "My good friend, Eleanor, if your eyes are good, your whole body will be full of light." He shakes his head at the others like a Mister-Know-It-All.

"William, since when do you read the *Good Book*?" Eleanor asks, actually wondering.

"As a matter of fact, I use it on a daily basis, especially when I write," he tells her, standing and then heading towards the Christmas tree.

Mary and Joe are watching him close. He lightheartedly throws back the words, "How do you think I won the Nobel Prize for Literature back in 1949? Couldn't get those Old Testament characters and the condition of their hearts out of my head. Then there's my writer's goods that I hope to get into the hands of somebody worth their salt someday."

"*Using* isn't the same as *reading*," Eleanor comments to Julius Caesar.

Joe feels compelled to say, "We go to the Firming Church of God in Meridian, Mississippi."

"And, who helped you think up the titles for some of your books, Billy?" Eleanor asks.

Faulkner ignores her.

Mary looks embarrassed when Mordecai holds up a bottle of Scotch whiskey.

Julius Caesar snarls again at Faulkner.

"Boy, the church house is for sinners. And even though I do qualify, I ain't about to go and let them ambush then crucify me like they have always relentlessly tried and ever wanted to do." Faulkner slides his eyes sideways to check on Mordecai. "Where's my Scotch?" Addressing Julius Caesar, "My Jacks would eat you alive!"

The cat ignores Faulkner. He walks over to Mordecai who has steadied himself on the refreshment cart with one hand and still holding a bottle of Scotch in his other hand. Faulkner gives him a nod to signal him to begin serving. He continues to the Christmas tree and solitarily begins decorating it from a box of ornaments on the floor. Mordecai begins to serve everyone in the parlor from a circle of polished silver cups.

"Mordecai, there's a bit of tepid fresh cream that I put on the cart for Julius Caesar along with his favorite Desert Rose saucer right beside that pretty green Depression glass fruit bowl that belonged to my mother," Eleanor explains. "Won't you see that he gets taken care of as well?"

Even though Mordecai is looking depressed, he manages to answer her with, "Certainly."

Eleanor smiles at Mary when Julius Caesar jumps up then shoots over to the cart for his cream. Joe investigates the back of the house with his eyes while thinking of Layne, and Mordecai, as dutiful as from the moment they first saw him, serves the Persian cat its cream.

Joe asks, "Mr. Faulkner, why do you write anyway?"

Mary cries out, "Joe, for God's sake, let the man have an evening where he doesn't have to think about writing, let alone books!"

Faulkner looks at Mary and says, "Little Lady, I have never had such an evening in my entire life! I expect folks to ask me questions. Why, I never stop thinking about writing not even during s-e-x!" He stops talking, walks over, takes a silver cup from Mordecai who turns to Mary and says, "But first things first, Sweet Mary. Will you kindly freshen up my Scotch with a little eggnog?"

His words confuse Mary. "Don't you mean to freshen your eggnog up with a little Scotch?"

She blushes when he says, "Neither does Tennessee Williams—stop thinking about s-e-x or writing or both—just ask him."

Joe asks, "Do you know Truman Capote?"

Faulkner replies with, "Don't get me started on his Other Voices *and their* Other Rooms or where—or what—his Miss Holly Golightly eats for breakfast!"

Julius Caesar stops drinking his cream and looks over at Eleanor who gives him a little wave of approval before entering the conversation. "I know why William writes."

Everyone turns and looks at her then to Faulkner.

It is Joe who says, "Well, I'm glad somebody knows!"

She nods.

William walks over and takes another ornament from the decoration box and hangs it on the tree. "It doesn't matter which way you do it, Sweet Mary. If you don't mind, pour me another shot of Scotch whiskey. And, Belladonna, I mean—Eleanor, tell me what's on your mind tonight, won't you?"

Eleanor smiles when Julius Caesar joins her on the settee. Waving at the fireplace, she says, "Mary, won't you give William one of my tea biscuits?"

"I ain't that particular. I can survive on my Scotch," he tells the tree.

Mary turns and sees Mordecai holding a bottle of Scotch whiskey in one hand and a sandwich tray of tea biscuits in the other. She takes both the bottle and the tray from him and serves Faulkner.

Mordecai turns and leaves the parlor.

"Did you get these at *Annabelle's Bakery* in Oxford?" Faulkner asks the tea biscuit.

"Indeed," Eleanor answers him.

He continues with, "Now, to answer Joe's question."

Everyone looks and sees Mordecai dragging a wooden stepladder into the parlor. He drags it over to where William is standing and leaves it open beside him. At first, William doesn't seem to notice the ladder. He lifts the African ivory star from the decoration box. He eyes the star curiously and walks over to place it on the coffee table near the Jerusalem Bible before he gulps another shot of Scotch.

Eleanor says, "William writes because what else would he do?"

Faulkner gives her a quizzical look. "Fair enough." He turns to Joe and says, "Joe, my boy, writing is hypnotic to my mind. It eases the pain within my soul. I write from my heart—for the most part—always have and always will *even though* I will die believing the human heart is always in conflict with itself." He pauses. "I never thought I had a damn thing to say either. If something came out that seemed contrived, I can assure you it was accidental. Some of my stories were real while some were imagined." He cups his chin between his thumb and pointer finger. "Believe it or not, the Bible has often served as my soul's tool of spiritual inspiration," he stops speaking. Then amid pure silence and anticipation he says, "And my neighbors."

Eleanor smiles to herself.

Joe asks, "Would you tell me more?"

Faulkner darts his eyes around the parlor, considers his thoughts, and continues with, "I think that if you want to be a writer you must write about things that come from the heart—universal truths—or not write at all. I have written sober. I have written drunk. I didn't let either state of mind stop me. I just wrote. That's all," he tells Joe. "I wanted to go to Harvard. I never made it but one of my characters did—briefly might I add." He laughs to himself before saying, "If you want to know the truth about it, I never got too much fancy education because I got kicked out of every school, I went to, in part, for writing my stories in class. Don't ever tell my baby girl, Jill, but I never passed too many tests either!"

Eleanor is startled by Faulkner's words and cries out, "Oh, my, William! Why, you ought to be ashamed of your bad self!"

Mary jumps, startled.

Faulkner smiles. He brushes the air with his right hand before saying to his hostess, "Shoot! Belladonna, I ain't ashamed of anything I ever did. *Are you?*"

Mordecai looks to Joe then to Eleanor while Mary looks from William to Eleanor who is reaching into her pocket.

Julius Caesar sneezes.

Eleanor puts on her dark spectacles.

Julius Caesar stands and whirls his head around at her, and then he sits back down.

"William, you are such a sincere liar," Eleanor comments.

"I deserved that," Faulkner tells her.

Eleanor goes inside herself. She snuggles herself into one comer of the settee. She pats Julius Caesar on the head until he purrs in grateful response.

Faulkner looks at Joe and says, "I did suffer a lot in my childhood and in my adult life. Sometimes I use my writing to ease the pain in my own conflicted heart. Still, I blame myself for certain *family matters...*"

Joe asks, "Mr. Faulkner, what about God? Do you believe in God?"

"Believe it or not, I am somewhat of a religious man. I guess you could say that I am a Believer if you want to *label* me. But Joe, my boy, don't you know—all writers go to hell? You can never trust a writer, especially when he's writing. I wrote from my heart. I guess that means my heart, like all of mankind, is full of darkness. Evil. Lies."

Joe jerks his neck back and nods once at Faulkner but says nothing.

He stops talking and takes notice of Joe's reaction. "Once a writer picks up a pencil, he's a liar."

Eleanor asks him, "William, what *do you* believe in?"

"Everything," Faulkner answers her adding, "The light; the darkness. Everything. I believe in everything, especially Scotch!"

Joe and Mordecai are both hanging onto Faulkner's every word.

Joe states, "We, Mary and I, that is, are Christians."

Faulkner snorts and laughs at Joe's words. Mordecai looks up at the oatmeal lid string hanging from the ceiling then towards the narrow hallway where he sees fresh footprints in a trail of lime that's coming from one of the other rooms.

Faulkner says, "Now, let me tell you—."

"Tell me," Joe interrupts.

"You so-called *Christians* are failing your Lord. And to tell the truth, Jews and total strangers are the only ones who have helped and believed in me over the years." Faulkner stops talking and appears to be thinking back.

Mordecai gets up and puts a stack of vinyl records on the talking machine and makes himself a drink.

Faulkner says, "Figure *that one* out. I can't. I am grateful, though, which is enough, I suppose."

Joe answers Faulkner with a stare.

Mordecai smiles to himself and sips on his drink.

"I am a Believer too," Eleanor states with regret in her voice. Everyone turns and looks at her when she confesses, "The good Lord knows I've failed Him and everyone else I know."

The song *Silver Bells* is filling the parlor from the talking machine.

"Aunt Eleanor, please don't talk like that! Take Layne for instance, he looks so good."

Mordecai gives Mary a bewildered look.

Faulkner smiles at everyone.

Eleanor asks, "When *did you* see Layne?"

"Oh, I saw a picture of him in one of the bedrooms," Mary lies.

"Which bedroom?" Eleanor asks, looking nervous.

Faulkner walks over from the coffee table and takes a bottle of Scotch whiskey from the refreshment cart and slips it into a comer of the decoration box. Then he takes some gold tinsel out of the box, unfolds it, climbs the ladder, and begins to drape it around the Christmas tree.

Eleanor checks Julius Caesar's neck watch against her own while he yawns.

"Mister Faulkner, would my Joe have to give up anything if he became a writer like you?" Mary asks.

Mordecai looks at Joe.

"Certainly not his goddamn Scotch whiskey! A writer's lone obligation in life is to his writing. Sweet Mary, Joe will have to be as mean as a rattlesnake then a sweet son-of-a-bitch *if he has to be* to make his own dream come true. Writing books for a living is a dream for most folks," he answers her while climbing down the ladder.

Eleanor nods then sighs.

Mordecai takes slow sips from his silver cup while Eleanor pats Julius Caesar's head.

"That's the way it is with any dream though," Faulkner says. With great thought he says, "The book will cause any writer pain like a goddamn woman in labor, I reckon you could say. The writer, like the woman, won't get a goddamn bit of relief until he is rid of his burden. Hell, he has to pop the book out of his mind—his skin even—like the woman has to pop the baby out of her body or else somebody dies," he tells them, reaching into the decoration box for his whiskey bottle. He pours himself another shot before he says, "No matter what, he can't let the book die. No peace, no sleep, no honor, little pride, no decency, no security, especially no happiness, until the book is finished, edited, and, of course, published. Why, a writer will rob his own mother if the need arises to make his dream come true!"

Eleanor gives Faulkner a sympathetic look.

He stops talking, gazes at Eleanor, and then continues, "That's why man needs God. God will give him the strength that he needs while he travails over his baby, his dream, his book, when no damn body else will!" Again, he stops talking but keeps his eyes focused straight on Eleanor's face before asking, "Ain't that right, Eleanor?"

Eleanor gives him a cool look and checks Julius Caesar's neck watch once again before saying, "I suppose."

"I believe you," Mordecai tells Faulkner.

Climbing the ladder, Faulkner first smiles at him then addresses Eleanor. "Did Edward throw himself into his mosaic wall or not? I know his writing in those goddamn memory books wasn't worth a dime. People that *fancy* themselves as a writer are typically the worst writers in the room. Now Hollywood has some great writers."

Mary gives Joe an appalled look.

Eleanor does not answer him; instead, she stretches out on the settee.

An anxious Mordecai speaks up. "I know I do! I've been trying for years to finish it. I can't seem to get it right. Something seems to slow me down."

Joe turns, offering him an encouraging smile.

"I can paint though," he adds, half smiling. "I painted a mural."

"Now that's the goddamn truth!" Faulkner shouts.

Mary is staring deeply at Mordecai—trying to figure him out.

Joe observes that Eleanor is still wearing her dark spectacles with Julius Caesar now lying on her stomach fast asleep.

Mary's eyes search around the parlor and into the hall before settling in a stationary stare on the Jerusalem Bible.

Faulkner nods then looks Joe's way inquiring in a fatherly tone, "Joe, my boy, would you rob your own mother if the need arose?"

Little Drummer Boy rings out of the talking machine.

"My mother is dead," Joe tells him in a sad voice.

"*Hildreth*," Mordecai announces with astonishment in his voice.

"What's that?" Faulkner asks, climbing down the ladder.

"I remembered that my mother's name was Hildreth," Mordecai says, turning towards Joe and Mary. Mordecai is smiling in reverie, "*She cared about me*—I remember the feeling of her touch. The look in her eyes before she walked toward the train with all the others leaving me alone but alive."

They both smile back at him. He closes his eyes as a state of luminous calm enters his face. Faulkner takes another swig from his whiskey bottle.

Eleanor looks puzzled by the conversation and cries out, "My goodness sakes alive—I didn't know you two were alone too!"

In support, Faulkner shrugs his shoulders at her.

Eleanor looks at Mordecai, and since he has his eyes closed, she thinks he's asleep.

Mary butts in with, "Yep, except for Joe's Paw, and he's just about drank himself half-crazy since his wife Jewel died from the Sugar Diabetes. Momma died the seventh day of March last year. I haven't had anybody to correspond with. She wrote to me all the time. Aunt Eleanor, did you know Daddy passed too in early October of last year?"

"No."

Mary's face saddens before she adds, "Joe and I love each other very much."

Faulkner looks up at the top of the Christmas tree, and he lets his eyes fall back to the oatmeal lid string hanging from the ceiling before confessing, "Sweet Mary, the Bible has always struck me as curious when I read the part about man being made in God's image. I have often thought that I was made in His shadow." He pours himself another shot of whiskey. "Maud, my momma, God rest her hard-headed soul, wrote me many letters over the years too. When I think back on it now, I believe that she got me in the habit of writing early on in life," he tells them. He hangs a small toy train on the tip of a branch.

Mary nods.

Mordecai opens his eyes.

Faulkner cocks his head in Mordecai's direction and yells, "Bring me another tea biscuit, you hear? They ain't half bad. But stay away from me with that goddamn shovel of yours, you hear?!"

Startled, Mordecai jumps up from his chair and obliges Faulkner who continues to decorate the Christmas tree alone. "Am I talking too goddamn much?" Faulkner asks the tree, actually wondering. Before he climbs back up the ladder, he takes a tea biscuit from the sandwich tray.

When Julius Caesar's neck watch alarms, Eleanor announces, "Time for my party!"

"Oh?" Mary asks.

While turning off Julius Caesar's watch alarm, she tells him, "We are going to have a party." She gives the Persian cat a hug, eliciting the purr of her beloved confidant.

"Belladonna, where did you get a watch that alarms?" Faulkner asked.

"Billy, now that's *our* secret," she replied, stroking her cat.

Faulkner frowned.

Mary remembers the snuff and gets up and walks over to where Eleanor is and slips the glass of mint-flavored snuff into her hand.

Eleanor looks alarmed until Mary whispers, "Happy Birthday. I love you."

With a jealous glare in his eyes, Julius Caesar moves away from them.

Eleanor smiles to herself, pops the metal top, and takes a dip of snuff with her pointer finger without noticing that Julius Caesar is now in a jealous snit with her.

Faulkner cries out, "Bring on the party!"

Mordecai smiles and reaches to pick up a little red glass candle in the shape of a rosebud. The unlit candle smells of pine. He reaches for a book of matches, opens the book, and strikes one then another until he lights the rosebud. When he places the two used matches back behind the unlit ones, he notices a carving of a fish chiseled into a stone-like pattern on the back of the match book.

Eleanor smiles when she sees the faint glow of the rosebud candle in the coffee table's green glass top. She reaches beneath the settee and brings back a little tin of sorts which she spits into. She takes off her dark spectacles, folds them, and puts them back in her pocket before asking, "Mordecai, would you mind bringing in our other guest for my party?"

"Certainly. After I bring in the cake," he answers.

"Oh, I forgot all about the cake!" Eleanor gets up and heads over to the same little table she'd looked at earlier near the narrow hallway. She opens its middle drawer and takes out an envelope.

Faulkner continues decorating the tree and climbs down the ladder like he's building a house. He soon nests a little lilac Victorian house with black trim with a wrap-around porch between two green branches of the Christmas tree.

Mary looks at Joe and says, "Looks like this is going to be a birthday night that we will always remember."

He nods and smiles with excitement.

Mordecai returns to the parlor with a German chocolate cake on a silver platter.

"Oh, it looks delicious!" Mary observes, making a place for the birthday cake on the coffee table.

Mordecai places the silver cake platter next to the Jerusalem Bible.

"Eleanor, are you going to let the boy out for Christmas or not?" Faulkner asks while climbing up and then down the ladder before he heads for the decoration box where he's secured himself another bottle of Scotch.

She doesn't reply. When her neighbor turns his whiskey bottle upside down and rudely takes another gulp, still, she isn't moved.

Instead, she stands in the narrow hallway with a dip of snuff in her bottom lip holding on tight to her envelope and whatever thoughts are in her mind.

NEWTON KNIGHT IS STANDING in front of the wall mosaic shaking his head when unexpectedly he walks through the wall where a fully dressed Layne is sitting on a red Verona Italian marble floor strumming a guitar. Books are scattered throughout the room. He reaches and picks up a *Life* magazine that has a photo of Elvis Presley on the cover. He attempts a half-smile before he chunks the magazine across the red Verona Italian marble floor. Knight walks back through the wall and stands in front of it, drops to his knees, and begins to fill in a corner section of it with pieces of dark-colored Venetian glass and brown colored stone, making the face of a Negro woman then creating a heart above her head with a piece of red Venetian glass. Once complete, he bows his head, stands, and wipes tears from his eyes and says, "Peace." He walks back through the now glowing mosaic wall.

Newton Knight is wearing a Confederate Southern Army uniform. The CSA uniform is worn and tattered with a bloodstain where his heart once was. Layne looks up and is so glad to see someone that he doesn't mind the morbid sight of the Confederate ghost.

Layne asks, "Who you?"

"I'm Newton Knight, and you?"

Layne smiles, stands, and announces, "I, Layne Edward Franklin."

"Pleased to meet you, Master Franklin," Knight tells him and offers him his hand.

Layne jumps up and shakes his hand like a refined man before asking, "You with Joe and Mary? I got dressed by myself."

Knight smiles, showing his rotten teeth and tells Layne, "I guess you might say that since Mary be the one who invited me here for Christmas Eve. Now it be this soldier's duty to thank her for allowing me to make peace with myself."

The word *Christmas* makes Layne feel uneasy. He cowers down in fear. "*Christmas?*"

"Almost Christmas, ain't it?" Knight asks Layne.

Layne ignores Knight's question, straightens his body back up, and asks, "You want to see my bird?"

"Shore. You got a bird in here?" Knight asks, rolling his eyes about the room.

Knight's interest excites Layne. He runs to his dresser, opens the third drawer, and stands looking like a proud father. Knight waits before walking over to the dresser. causing Layne to cry out, "Come over here. Hurry up! Would you?"

Knight obliges him. When he looks inside the dresser drawer, he sees pieces of broomstraw and threads of twine. Sitting right in the middle of it all is a little sparrow. Brightly colored tissue wallpapers three sides of the drawer, and an old, faded photograph turned around covers the last wall of the drawer. There is a small red apple, a rabbit's foot on a shiny metal key ring, and rocks of various sizes surrounding a tunnel made of shittim wood. Near the opening of the tunnel sits a rusty canning jar lid filled with water. Beneath the rusty lid is an old piece of paper partly faded by time, but still legible is, "Fancy Cherries are Florida's *Red* Sunshine."

Knight says, "Would you look at that?"

Layne reaches deep into the back of his dresser drawer and brings back an almost completely faded piece of thin paper and hands it to Knight.

Knight gives Layne a curious look when he cries out, "Have this!"

After taking the piece of paper from Layne, Knight shrugs and hands it back to Layne who reads aloud, "Romans 8:28, Holy Bible." Knight reaches and takes the piece of paper from Layne and places it into the open hole in his chest. Layne looks surprised when Knight reaches into his drawer for a crayon portrait of William Faulkner takes it, folds it, and places it into his chest as well.

Layne smiles and asks, "Did you bring any cheese? My bird likes cheese."

"Nope. What's his name?"

Layne begins stroking the sparrow's back before he affectionately says, "JoJo."

Knight reaches into his pocket and pulls out a piece of paper that catches Layne's eye with its magical glow. One side of the paper looks like a dollar bill while the other side is a brilliant, golden orange.

"You going to give me that dollar?" Layne asks. His eye widens.

Knight doesn't answer Layne. He smiles, lifts the piece of paper to his nose, closes his eyes, and takes a deep whiff as if it is a golden rose.

ELEANOR IS STANDING near the coffee table with an envelope in her hand. Faulkner is walking around admiring his decorating of the Christmas tree while Mary and Joe are sitting on the couch sipping eggnog from their silver cups. The rosebud candle continues to fill the parlor with the scent of pine burning brightly from the coffee table.

"Mary, can we finish our previous conversation before the other guest arrives?" Eleanor asks.

"What about the others?" Mary asks.

"My soul has waited in silence for so long. I'm ready to have my say."

Mary looks at Joe who nods.

Faulkner says, "Talk on."

"Thank you kindly, William. My heart has been in my land and the wealth that it has had to offer me for the last twenty years. Maybe even longer."

"Why, whatever do you mean?" Mary asks.

Eleanor wipes snuff juice from the corners of her mouth with her thumb and index fingers. "Mary, I own hundreds of acres besides the twenty-nine where Fable Court sits. I've had a sign posted for years offering "free land" to folks, but I have never given as much as a single acre to anyone who stopped by in their cars—who served as my occasional guests. Not to a single soul have I given an acre too!"

Faulkner gives her a sharp look as if to say, *Are you sure you want to keep talking?*

She nods at him and continues with, "I must confess, I was lonely and greedy. I want to make peace with the Lord before another year passes on by me."

"Aunt Eleanor, now please don't talk that way!" Mary cries out.

Faulkner sits down on the floor beside the now empty decoration box and cocks his left ear Eleanor's way. He cuts his eyes towards a whiskey bottle in a corner of the box and lets out a long breath of air from his nose before he mumbles, "Alas, digging up an old well. We all do it."

Mary is shocked and upset by her aunt's words. She turns to Joe for comfort, but he's looking down the narrow hallway towards Mordecai's room.

"It's true," Eleanor tells her niece. She stops speaking, closes her eyes, cocks her neck back then forward a couple of times, and rolls her neck around on her shoulders before saying, "Mary, some twenty-odd years ago, I did an awful thing. It's time the truth was let out."

Joe gives the parlor the once-over, settling a stare on Eleanor.

The temperature begins to drop in Oxford.

Mary asks, "What in the world do you mean? I thought we were going to talk about Uncle Edward. What have you got on your mind from over twenty years ago?"

Eleanor stands, walks over to another couch, and sits down between Joe and Mary. She reaches into her pocket and pulls out her dark spectacles.

"Oh, me," Faulkner says to the Christmas tree when Bing Crosby singing *White Christmas* pours from the talking machine.

Eleanor puts on her dark spectacles.

"Excuse me?" Joe asks Faulkner.

William shakes his head at the Christmas tree but says nothing. He gets up and continues to decorate it with colorful balls.

"Oh, Mary, it was my birthday. Layne and I had been in the kitchen all day long cooking and having a ball together. I had given all the Negroes the day off so that we three could have a little family party of our own."

Joe smiles at Mary when she hears Bing Crosby's voice ring out from the talking machine.

Eleanor drops her head forward and exhales. When she lifts her head back up, she looks so exasperated that Mary puts her hand on one of her knees. Joe moves in closer to her other side surrounding her with family comfort.

Faulkner goes for another bottle of Scotch whiskey off the refreshment cart.

"Now, that does sound like you all were going to have a big time! Doesn't it, Joe?" Mary says, hoping to encourage her aunt because she is looking more depressed than ever.

No answer from Joe. Instead, he musters up the kindest face he can in hopes to offer some comfort to this old, frail, depressed woman who, by writing them one letter, came so quickly into their lives that they hardly saw it happen.

"Crack!" Faulkner breaks the seal on another bottle of Scotch whiskey.

"It was supposed to be a big time, but it was far from it, so far, my dear Mary—so far," Eleanor says before her mind drifts. When she can collect her thoughts, she continues with, "Mary, I've known for a long time that my mind is in a state of constant change, but I didn't know what to do. Ever since I moved to Mississippi, all I ever had was my Edward. Then, dear, sweet Layne came late in our lives, and he got the measles. He and I were never to be the same." She stops talking, setting her eyes on the rosebud candle's flickering flame. "Edward blamed me for everything that went wrong in our lives, including the effects the measles had on Layne. To this day, I don't know why they affected him like they did..." Her words trail off, she pauses, and then says with finality, "But they did."

"You mean, why Edward thought they left the boy retarded?" Faulkner blurts out.

Everyone in the parlor ignores Faulkner's frankness.

Mary is alarmed by what she is hearing so she asks, "Why in the world would Uncle Edward blame you for Layne's condition, let alone everything that went wrong in your lives?"

"After we were married, he became bitter, angry, and cold towards me. Unless he wanted something, well, you know—the husband and wife union—from me. When I couldn't keep him satisfied, that's when he bought the White House just outside the south gate of the then University of Mississippi campus." She pauses, takes a deep breath, and says, "Poppa warned me not to marry him. We used to have a lighthouse and lived on the sea somewhere in New England. Poppa told me that the lighthouse had a great lens on top that had a magic light that focused on enemy ships and set them ablaze. True or not, I believed him."

"I don't blame you for believing, Eleanor. Rail on," Faulkner blurts out.

"The lighthouse wasn't just for guiding ships. It was above a secret tomb. Its light was *ours* to use to guard off the souls of the dead that were wandering aimlessly over the sea. Mary, the lighthouse always made me, and your mother, feel lonely and uncertain about life in the world outside of ours. We only had our books and our diaries to keep us company until we lost our library in a fire. We did manage to save some of our diaries from the flames though."

"Momma never told me about a lighthouse or a fire," Mary muses. "Oh, how beautiful it all sounds! Why did you marry Uncle Edward then? I mean, if you had such a life in New England, why trade it for Mississippi?"

"*Enemy ships?*" Faulkner asks the Christmas tree. Julius Caesar looks over at him when he adds, "Eleanor, I want you to tell them about the goddamn pear tree."

"Love," Eleanor tells everyone with earnest while hugging herself.

"Pear tree?" Joe asks.

Faulkner gives him a tight smile before blurting out, "Eleanor, tell us more about the about the White House, won't you?"

Julius Caesar snarls over at Faulkner.

"Of course, you were in love. How stupid of me to overlook that! Now, don't you be so hard on yourself; you hear?" Mary says in a comforting voice.

"Yes, I needed his love—anybody's love—after what Poppa did to me all those years. I never told Momma. She was the most beautiful woman—inside and out—in my world. Momma never seemed to age. From the beginning, I didn't even know what s-e-x was for. When

I didn't even give Edward a baby after all those years, he bought the White House. Almost daily he threw it in my face that I wasn't anything without him, the land, the money and, and, and the University of Mississippi!"

Faulkner raises his eyebrows.

Joe listens.

Astounded by her aunt's bluntness, Mary asks, "Uncle Edward said that to you? Aunt Eleanor, what White House do you mean?"

"Outside the south gate of the campus there is a White House with four pillars across its front that Edward bought and pretended to rent it out to young, good-looking, wholesome college boys. Believe you me, no rent money of significance was ever exchanged!"

Mary interrupts with, "Oh no! Aunt Eleanor, are you sure you want to talk about all of this in front of everyone?"

Eleanor declares, "You and Joe are my family—and William is no less. Besides, I'm feeling better already by talking to someone other than Julius Caesar."

"If you want to talk all night, that's fine by me. Hell, it's your birthday! You got my vote to say, do, and act whatever way you goddamn well please!" Faulkner yells out.

Joe nods at everyone.

With affection, "Thank you, Billy," Eleanor says to her neighbor.

"Go on. Tell us about the rent money; then tell them about the goddamn pear tree," Faulkner encourages her.

"S-e-x," she spells, and taps the rim of her dark spectacles.

"*Sex?*" Mary says.

"That's what she said," Faulkner puts in and raises his eyebrows.

"Instead of Edward collecting money for rent, the boys were *his boys* to do what he pleased to and with!"

Mary gasps.

"Why did you put up with that?" Joe asks.

"Charles Edward Franklin *was* a good looking fellow," Faulkner muses and takes another drink of Scotch. "I didn't know that he was a sweet son-of-a-bitch though! Maybe he was not a marrying man to begin with..."

"Maybe," Joe echoed him.

"L-o-v-e. Edward was the only man I'd ever known besides Poppa. I loved him from the center of my heart. I thought he was going to help me escape Poppa and all. I married him to get away from Poppa."

"Oh, no, you don't mean *what* I think you mean, do you?!" Mary questions her aunt.

"*Goddamned sin-damaged before she left the nest,*" Faulkner mumbles.

"Why didn't you pray to God to change Uncle Edward's heart?" Mary asks her.

"Why ask God to change somebody He created in His image?" Eleanor replies.

Mary gives her aunt and then Joe a shocked look.

"She's got a point," Faulkner offers.

"I don't believe that for a minute!" Mary tells them.

"Babydoll, stay out of it," Joe cautions.

"God was watching everything Poppa then Edward did to me. He didn't stop either one of them. Or take away my pain. God was of no use to me. If He was, I didn't know it," she tells everyone.

"Aunt Eleanor, if you want God to get involved in your mess, I mean your life, you've got to *ask* for His help," Mary tells her. "God cannot help you if you don't ask. *You got to ask!*"

"Mary, please let her be now. She did what she thought was right at the time," Joe says.

"I was too weak and insecure and ashamed and afraid to speak up. I never knew that love and pain were one and the same until I married," she talks on.

"I don't feel that way at all, do you Joe?" Mary asks Joe.

"No," he replies.

"When I got 'that way,' with Layne..." Eleanor begins.

It is Faulkner who chooses to translate, "Pregnant."

"Edward no longer wanted to have me near him. He'd leave any room in Fable Court when I entered."

Joe puts his arm across the back of the couch.

Faulkner gives them a tight smile.

"After teaching Shakespeare and Latin all day, Edward would often come home, and I would be sitting in this very parlor waiting with a pot of piping hot tea before he'd burst the pot into a million bits. Tea and sugar and cream would be all over the parlor. I'd have to clean it up otherwise, it would still be there for you to see. He would *never* have cleaned it up! He was *that* stubborn. He was mean to me. My own husband could go an entire year without saying one word to me."

"Oh, my Lord in heaven!" Mary cries out.

"He'd even get angry with me about the tea biscuits."

"*Tea biscuits?*" Faulkner asks.

"Oh, yes! Edward wanted a slice of German chocolate cake, *not* tea biscuits."

"Peculiar," Mary tells Joe who nods.

"His eyes would blacken. He'd go into a rage and break my Desert Rose teacups and stalk out of Fable Court, but not without telling me I was nothing without him and fat and pregnant with a bad seed growing inside me. That my genes were bad because of Poppa's love for the whiskey bottle. He would say that if he could have one wish come true in this world it would be that *my* baby be born dead because he didn't need *two* nothings *imposed* on him. Edward said I was 'imposed' on him. My husband and that he never wanted to marry me anyway. For years, I became so confused that I couldn't even think straight!"

"You didn't believe him, did you?" Mary asks.

"You always believe the one you love, especially when you are all alone. That is, until one day I remembered I had kept some of my diaries and my own memory books. I searched them and found out that I had never 'imposed' myself on him at all. That's when I learned to love and hate him at the same time."

Mary gasps and reaches over and hugs her aunt.

Eleanor continues with, "One afternoon after Edward had broken my Desert Rose teacups, he ran out and, I asked one of our hired hands, JoJo, to take me in his pickup truck to find him. We ended up at the White House. I told JoJo to wait in the truck for me while I went inside to talk some sense into my husband. The front door was ajar, so I went on inside and found no one. I decided to walk around the White House and pick me a few figs off the tree in the back yard. Funny thing, I craved figs while I was pregnant with Layne. After I'd picked myself half-a-dozen big, ripe, juicy figs, I heard someone moaning and groaning and making sounds like they were riding a horse. I walked a ways into the woods behind the White House, and that's when I saw my husband with his pants down below his knees and his hands around the waist of a young handsome boy who was on his knees in a red velvet high-back, Victorian turn-of-the century chair and holding on tight to the red-velvet high-back chair. Like a horse, Edward was shoving himself into his behind while saying, 'Yes! Yes! Yes!'"

"Oh, hell no!" Faulkner yells.

Mary goes to console her aunt, but Eleanor cries out, "Leave me be!"

Mary asks, "Joe?"

"Leave her be," Joe tells Mary.

Mary asks, "How could you face him, let alone sleep with him after that?"

"I couldn't. He didn't want me anyway. He never *truly* wanted me. I could always *feel* it."

"I guess the holy hell not," Faulkner comments, taking another swig of Scotch.

"I'll never forget that day. JoJo never knew about what I saw. I shared my figs with him on the way back to Fable Court. As we drove along Garfield Road, I began crying, and when JoJo asked me what was wrong, I told him I was happy because I could feel my baby kicking and that I knew it wouldn't be long until I had someone of my very own to hold and love. I went into labor that self-same afternoon. Edward never knew what I saw either."

Silence.

"JoJo took me to the hospital, and I went on and gave birth to Layne who was the joy of my life from the very first moment I saw him. No one was with me when he was born. I kept Edward away from him as much as I could for fear of what he might do to him. He never wanted much to do with him anyway, so he didn't put up a fight. I'd get weak and hunger for, even crave, some family l-o-v-e on holidays though. Like I said, one year it was my birthday and Layne, and I had baked a German chocolate cake. Why, I had even ordered myself some *Fancy Cherries* from Florida." Eleanor pauses and gathers more thoughts before saying, "We were carrying it into where Edward was in his library. He was always such a fool about William Shakespeare. He was ashamed that Layne couldn't understand it, not to mention how Layne had taken to the Negroes. Sometimes Edward acted like he wanted a son. But when Layne would start to laugh and talk, he would just fly into a rage and curse me for being alive and having him. I felt like a Nobody—invisible." She stops talking and looks further back in time. "I thought he would die from a heart attack because he would get so mad when he drove up and Layne was outside playing with the Negro children. Then, one time he beat Layne so badly that I had to doctor the whelps and sores that his own father put on his back for weeks!"

Mary gasps.

"Layne didn't even know why he was being whipped," Eleanor says, holding her head down before confessing, "I believe that my Layne often thought he was a Negro."

"Oh, my goodness!" Mary cries out.

Joe jerks his neck around, and then hits the arm of the couch.

Faulkner spits out the words, "That goddamn son-of-a-bitch, low-down coward!"

O Come, O Come, Emmanuel drops onto the talking machine.

Eleanor is offended by Faulkner's words, so she tells him, "Billy, now he was my husband. So, don't go calling him names. Hear?"

Faulkner backs off with his name-calling and says, "I'm sorry." He walks over and opens the window a little and urges a spider on outside into the cold night. Then he cries out, "Even pure meanness can cause a man to forget he's a man! He was a low-down coward to do that to you and to the boy—and, and, and to himself!"

Eleanor reaches behind her dark spectacles and wipes at her eyes. "Billy, he was all I had—low-down coward or not!"

"Let's talk about something else! Mister Faulkner, please tell Joe some more about your writing," Mary insists and looks around the parlor searching for words to say before reaching into her pocket and pulling out the piece of wood.

Joe gives her a serious look.

Eleanor senses the panic in her voice. "Mary, please let me finish what it has taken me years to start. Billy and Joe can talk after I've had my say."

"*O come, O come, Emmanuel, / And ransom captive Israel, / That mourns in lonely exile here / Until the Son of God appear. /*

"That's right, sweet Mary," Faulkner puts in.

"Rejoice! Rejoice! Emmanuel / shall come to thee, O Israel." whirls out from the talking machine.

Joe motions for Mary to be silent. She begins to pat her lips with the piece of wood.

Faulkner gives them an exasperated look before saying, "Rail on Eleanor! Rail on!"

"Never giving up hope that Edward would see we loved him, in the hazy shade of winter one day Layne and I made a German chocolate cake that he always asked for on my birthday. I'd topped it with the cherries I'd ordered from Florida. After we'd taken a picture of it, we were bringing it into this very parlor for Edward to cut the first piece. We didn't know he was in a bad mood. We were singing. Layne loved to sing. He learned many a gospel song from the Negroes. Edward jumped up and started in on Layne and me ganging up on him. He said that I had made a sissy out of Layne because I had taught him to cook. He accused me of conspiring to poison not only the birthday cake but his only son against him!"

Mary lifts her hands and covers her ears.

Faulkner turns one of his Scotch whiskey bottles straight up.

Eleanor stops talking for a few seconds and catches her breath. "Like a little hurt child, Layne began to fret and cry, which set Edward into one of his blind rages. He jumped up and knocked the birthday cake out of my hands."

Mary uncovers her ears. "Oh, Lord no!" she cries out and instinctively closes her eyes as if to keep from seeing what's to come.

"I had hold of the butcher knife that was beneath the cake plate. Well, before I knew it, I was stabbing and stabbing and stabbing. I was so angry that I couldn't even see straight! All I could see was a deep darkness absent from any light whatsoever while I screamed and stabbed all about the parlor. Although I can't remember what words I was screaming, I'm sure Layne heard every word of it. When I came to myself, I saw that I had stabbed my Edward eight times or more. Layne had fainted on the floor. I knew one thing to be true though — I'd taken away my husband's birthday on mine."

Mary gasps. She is holding her forehead with her left hand.

Joe says, "Damn!"

"When I tried to help Layne, I saw that he had lost his right eye in the struggle. I ran out back to the shack where JoJo and Clara lived and asked him to come take care of Layne until I could get the parlor cleaned up." Eleanor gives the rosebud candle flame a glance. She reaches over and picks up the Jerusalem Bible and says, "Jojo swore on this here Bible that he would never tell a soul save for Clara. That dear Negro man kept his word to me. If he told Clara, she never once let on to me that she knew a thing."

Faulkner's look is so penetrating that it appears his eyes might burn a hole through Eleanor.

Joe's face is pale.

Mary still has her eyes closed.

Joe speaks, "Who else knows about this?"

"Just JoJo and Layne. JoJo passed on about ten year ago. Mary's momma came to know it too," she tells Joe, and then she looks at Faulkner before adding, "I did manage to keep a diary though."

Faulkner smiles at her.

"What did you do after you came to yourself?" Joe asks.

Faulkner shakes his head in disbelief.

"I dragged him into his closet. Quickly, I took off my best housecoat and threw it into the fireplace to burn," she answers and gazes into an empty fireplace.

Joe waits.

"And, like I said earlier, I took Layne out back to JoJo's place and told him to look after Layne until I let him know otherwise. I believe his old lady, Clara, made cheese for her egg money because they had a house full of children to feed. I told another Negro to take a horse and go fetch young Sheriff Delk. When Sheriff Delk came, I told him that Layne and I had surprised an intruder or maybe even an escaped convict from the Mississippi State Penitentiary who had murdered my husband and he had run out after stabbing my son and having his way with me. He never asked me another question about it after that day," she tells them.

"I'm not surprised," Faulkner mutters under his breath. "That good-for-nothing, so-called goddamn lawman—young or old—was never worth a hill of beans anyway!"

"Oh, my Lord in heaven! My *Momma knew*?" Mary wails out and opens her eyes before she asks, "What about Layne's eye?"

Eleanor struggles with an answer until she says, "That's the worst part—."

Mary gasps.

Eleanor hangs her head in shame before confessing, "I haven't been able to face Layne in all these years knowing I couldn't give him his right eye or his father back. I kept using the excuses that the wall mosaic or that the writings in the memory books wasn't finished. Truth be told, I am the low-down coward in Fable Court."

Joe says, "Then I will say it: It is finished!"

Eleanor looks stunned.

Mary shouts, "Oh, Aunt Eleanor! Why in the world didn't you let some of us look after Layne?"

"For one thing, Layne always reminded me of Poppa. After I had realized that I had done such a thing to Edward and to him, I knew that I could never look him in the face again, nor could I tell anyone else what I'd done. My mind was muddled."

Faulkner looks over at her and then back to the Christmas tree and comments, "Eleanor, I agree with Joe. That goddamn wall mosaic is as good as it's ever going to get. Why you've not seen it in years. Edward's story will never change. Those memory books — I know what to do with them — just give them to me for Christmas. Damn it to hell, Eleanor! Now, please let the boy out!"

She ignores Faulkner's words and says, "As the years passed, I fell into such a state of love-hate solitary living. I know I've caused everyone including myself such terrible pain and eternal grief. I don't know why, but I never could forget what Poppa did to me in the secret hours of the night when everyone at Belladonna was asleep. I suppose being alone too much gave me too much time to think about the past because there was no future for me to look forward to anymore at Fable Court. When Edward's promise of love didn't make it, all go away, I didn't know what to do with my love-hate then or now. Truth be told, I'm too old now to change."

Everyone looks on speechless while Eleanor stares straight at the Christmas tree and begins to softly sing, *"I'm just a needless old woman ending my song. That, like a wounded snake, I've dragged myself slowly along..."*

The talking machine clicks off. And, at once, everyone in the parlor knows she is telling the truth of the matter.

When Mary begins to cry, Eleanor says, "Layne used to have crying spells too. Yes, crying spells. I'd talk to him through the wall mosaic for hours, sometimes read the Bible and other great books from the Reading Room to him."

"That was good of you," Faulkner comments.

"That's the worst thing I've ever of heard in all of my life!" Mary wails, tears streaming down her cheeks.

Joe slides his eyes over to the narrow hallway like he's heard something or someone.

Faulkner cries out, "You can't go back, Eleanor! Goddamn it to hell, none of us can! God can't even go back."

Joe nods and wipes his eyes.

"Billy, I know the dreams I once had were shattered the day I ran away and married Charles Edward Franklin. It isn't because of Mississippi or Ole Miss. The soul of the man I married was never free to love me." She stops talking. "I'm *so tired* of feeling rejected, unwanted and unloved. Starting each day with yesterday and no tomorrow in sight is an awful way to live."

Faulkner interrupts, "Eleanor, that's not living!"

Her face takes on the vague resemblance to one of those angels seen in church windows—sort of tragic—scared even before she holds up the envelope that she's been clutching and says, "Mary, I want you and Joe to take this letter to Judge Fenton Van Buren Stringer on Monday. It has been notarized by my lawyer, Fenton's twin brother, Laurel Stringer, and signed by me. It states that I'm signing everything that I own over to you two except for my diaries and any memory books found in Fable Court. They go to my neighbor and friend, Billy Faulkner—William Faulkner, that is. You can move into Fable Court now if you wish or you can wait until the good Lord calls my name and I join my Edward—whenever that may be."

Mary and Joe exchange glances.

Joe gives Eleanor a nod of approval.

"Now, there is one stipulation to my wishes—that you two have to look after Layne until he dies. I left Mordecai well-provided for too."

"You didn't tell them about the goddamn pears," Faulkner urges her, reaches over, and opens the window further. He looks outside. "It's snowing in Oxford. Holy hell! It looks like we are going to have a white Christmas after all."

Eleanor nods at Faulkner. "The first weekend of September, and before all this happened, Layne and I had been gathering pears off his Kieffer pear tree. He loved the outdoors and growing things. It was loaded down. You should have seen it. Clara came over and helped us put up a few jars. Why, she even brought some of her own canning lids because I ran out, and I couldn't drive a lick. Then I copied down little Scripture messages from the Holy Bible about heaven to go along with the canned pears. Layne wrapped them in bright tissue paper for Christmas gifts for the Negroes. We had the best time until Edward found out about it. He must have gone out late that very night because the next morning Layne came running into the kitchen upset and pointing towards the window yelling, 'Look! Just look!' When I looked out the window, I saw that someone had severed the arms off Layne's pear tree. There they lay on the ground—still loaded down with pears. Layne never did get over that. He got so upset that he ran into the pantry and started busting up the jars of canned pears. Indeed, Layne had a temper like the rest of us at Fable Court. Edward whipped him good and made him clean up the mess—alone—and drag the cut limbs into the ditch, cover them with broom straw, dash the pile with kerosene, and set fire to the lot of it. Layne cried himself to sleep many a night because of it," Eleanor covers her face and says, "As did I."

"Oh, how cruel!" Mary cries out and reaches for her aunt, but Eleanor gets up from her place between Mary and Joe and walks over to the settee and stretches herself out.

Joe shakes his head in disbelief.

Faulkner staggers over to the refreshment cart and begins puttering around like a lost old man in need of a bed and a good night's sleep, not another bottle of Scotch whiskey.

Julius Caesar stretches his neck and looks towards Faulkner when he blurts out the question, "Eleanor, where's the goddamn lights for the Christmas tree?"

No answer.

Eleanor begins to sob on the settee when Mary challenges her heart with the words, "Aunt Eleanor, why you can't leave us everything. What about Layne? Don't you even want to see your own son again?"

She doesn't answer Mary. She gets up, walks over to the coffee table, picks up the rosebud candle, and blows it out while hugging herself she is saying, "I'm cold now. I'm tired too. I waited until you came. Don't cha know that you two are all the family I have left in this world to come for my birthday?"

Joe looks at the German chocolate cake and asks, "Oh mercy, mercy, mercy me! All right let's have a party! If it's a party that will make you happy, then someway, somehow by God, we will oblige! Is Mordecai going to bring Layne in for the party or not? Is he waiting for you to give the word? Is that why he's taking so long?"

"Why, I *never* even considered it," Eleanor says and takes another dip of snuff.

THE NORTH WINDOW in Layne's room is long and narrow and covered by a once high fashion window shade. Newton Knight walks over and jerks twice on the shade's tassel which causes it to spin. Layne watches him while smiling up at the spinning shade. Knight beckons him with a hand gesture to look outside. Layne obliges Knight and is surprised by the night's snow. It startles him. He rubs at his right eye which causes blood to drip out from behind the corner of his black leather eye patch.

Layne cries out, "Look! Ahhh, the sky is crying!"

Newton Knight nods his head in agreement.

Layne marvels, shakes his head, and confesses, "I know crying, I know crying. I know crying..."

Knight smiles and takes him by the hand and says, "Master Layne, come with me."

Layne lets go of Knight's hand long enough to walk over and get his guitar. Then he shoves the sparrow into his pocket along with an old photograph that he grabs from his dresser drawer. Although Layne doesn't know Knight, he senses that something good is about to happen, so he looks up at Knight and says, "I sing."

"What can you sing?" Knight asks him.

"Elvis teach me to sing! And Mordecai," he tells Knight.

"What's an *Elvis*?" Knight asks, and Layne gives him a puzzled look when together they walk through the completed glowing wall mosaic of *The Loaves and Fishes—the Power and Presence*.

Layne looks back at the glowing mosaic and says to Knight, "I like fish. Julius love fish! My bird love fish too. Billy asked me what I like besides cheese, and I says, 'I like fish!' Billy says, 'Okay! We make a fish one like in the Bible.' Billy let me make a fish one by myself. I love that Billy! He gave me a Bible picture book."

Knight nods but doesn't speak.

Everyone in the front parlor, but Faulkner, looks up to see Newton Knight and Layne walking into the room. Both are smiling. Faulkner is holding the African ivory star in his hand and trying to figure out how to get it on top of the Christmas tree.

Julius Caesar meows, and then he snarls at the Confederate ghost.

Mary jumps to her feet and starts towards them, but Joe signals her to stay put by fanning his hand in the air. She catches Joe's signal and sits back down on the edge of the couch.

"Mordecai, would you please bring in our guest now?!" Eleanor cries out.

Julius Caesar meows again like he's part of the conversation.

Mary can hardly believe what she's seeing and shakes her head as if to clear it.

"Hush up Julius Caesar—can't you see it's almost my birthday?" Eleanor tells her Persian cat in a scolding voice. The tone of her voice causes him to go into a snit with her. He gives her a sullen look and retreats underneath the settee into one of his morose moods.

Layne smiles over at William Faulkner like an old friend and says, "Hey, Billy."

Faulkner smiles then waves before saying, "Hello, Layne. Good to see you, my boy!"

"Oh, my God! Joe—just look!" Mary cries out.

Still wearing her dark spectacles, Eleanor stands, spits her snuff out behind the settee, and to all outward appearances ignores Layne.

Layne's right eye is bleeding. He wipes it with his shirt sleeve. He smiles at Joe and says, "Joe? That you, Cousin Joe?"

"Hey, hotshot! You going to play us a Christmas song on that guitar of yours?" Joe asks him and claps his hands over his head in the twelve o'clock position.

Layne spots Eleanor and runs over towards her shouting, "Momma, Momma, Momma! Where you been?!"

Eleanor is grasping at her ears with her hands and rolling her head like a spinning top. "What say? Did somebody call my name?" Eleanor asks, grasping both ears, "Mordecai? Where are you?"

Mordecai's groan can be heard from within the narrow hallway like a bolt of thunder.

Eleanor lies back down on the settee and covers her ears with her hands.

Julius Caesar peeps out from underneath the settee, and then he crawls out.

Layne senses that something is wrong and stops in the middle of the parlor to play his guitar before he gets to Eleanor.

Joe stands, then he sits back down.

Layne begins to sing and play the song *Silent Night* on his guitar. At first, he sings the words slowly, *"Holy, holy night."* With great effort he sings, *"Holy night, calm is all, all is bright*—No!" he yells at himself. He stops to clear his throat. He tries to sing in the best voice that he can muster up.

Joe and Mary begin to cry.

Faulkner is still holding the African ivory star and steps back from the Christmas tree to watch. To listen.

Layne wipes at the blood coming from behind his right-eye black leather patch with the elbow of his shirt sleeve before continuing. *"Silent night, holy night! / All is calm, all is bright / All is sleeping while lonely Layne watches no one / Sleep in heavenly peace / Sleep in heavenly peace...*

Eleanor acts like her only son is invisible.

From the narrow hallway, Mordecai enters the parlor pushing a red velvet high-back, Victorian turn-of-the century chair with the decomposed, rotted-to-the-core body of Charles Edward Franklin surrounded by yellow-green pears.

Layne begins singing in German, *"Stille Nacht, heilige Nacht, / Alles schlaft; einsam wacht / Nur das traute hochheilige Paar. / Holder*

Knabe im lockigen Haar, / Schlaf in himmlischer Ruh! / Schlaf in himmlischer Ruh!"

"...Stille Nacht, heilige Nacht, / Hirten erst kundgemacht / Durch der Engel Halleluja, / Tont es laut von fern und nah: / Christ, *der Retter ist da! /* Christ, *der Retter ist da!"*

Mary screams.

Joe jumps to his feet and yells, "Mordecai, what in God's name have you gone and done?!"

Mordecai gives an eternal groan.

Momentarily astonished, Faulkner is standing amid the Franklins and the Farmers, unbeknownst to him, holding Hemingway's African ivory star and looking shocked and, strangely enough, now slightly sober.

When Layne notices the Christmas tree, he gasps in excitement, drops his guitar, and startles Julius Caesar. When he sees the German chocolate cake, he begins to sing the, *Happy Birthday* song.

Layne turns and sees Mordecai pushing Edward's body. He reaches for the chocolate cake, and when he knocks it over, the butcher knife falls to the floor. Instinctively, he reaches for it. Eleanor stands to greet her beloved guest, Charles Edward Franklin. Still, she is bent on ignoring her only son. Layne runs over to her and begins stabbing and stabbing at her little frail body while shouting, "Yes! Yes! Yes! I love you! I love you! I love you!"

Mary screams.

"Holy Mother of God! Joe, stop him!" Faulkner yells while running towards Eleanor who isn't making a sound. But it is too late. Eleanor falls to the floor as limp as a bloody wet rag.

"No, Layne! No! No! No!" Mary screams.

At once, he drops the butcher knife and starts drooling out of one corner of his mouth. He hands Mary the photograph. Stunned, she looks at the last living photograph of Layne and Eleanor—the family together, smiling, sharing a piece of German chocolate cake covered with red cherries at another birthday party.

Mary screams, "Oh, my God! No! Joe!"

Unmoved and without reason for his stabbing of Eleanor, Layne reaches into his pocket and comes back with a little sparrow and shouts, "See, JoJo? He likes cheese!"

With the African ivory star in hand, William Faulkner lunges at Layne and trips, falling on top of Edward's decomposed and rotted body. When Mordecai scrambles to help him off the body, it breaks into a million pieces.

"Goddamn it to hell!" Faulkner yells, dropping the African ivory star amid the broken body of Charles Edward Franklin that's emitting a dark smoke, that is filling the parlor.

In cupped hands, Layne holds up the sparrow and releases it towards the Christmas tree. When it begins to fly in an overpowering fright around the parlor, he calls out, "JoJo, we not lonely no more! Fly! Fly! Fly!"

Mary screams to the top of her voice.

Joe yells, "Layne, no!"

"Not me! I not lonely no more!" Layne says to the ceiling, not realizing that the cat will go for the bird. When Layne sees Julius Caesar become alert and stiffen his body in the direction of JoJo and getting into a springing position, he grabs the Jerusalem Bible from the coffee table and throws it at the cat, knocking it out cold. A calling card with Revered Morty Rayborn's name on it flies from the Jerusalem Bible onto a Persian carpet near one end of the settee. The glass jar of mint-flavored snuff rolls out from Eleanor's eternal grasp and joins the card on the Persian carpet.

With eyes like moonlight on ice, Newton Knight glides by everyone and stops beside Eleanor. He reaches into bloodstain where his heart once was and pulls out a silver slate that is gleaming with bezel-set sapphires. The Confederate ghost turns and hands the silver slate to a staggering William Faulkner who turns it over and reads aloud from its backside, "Truth can stand alone in any light—but more so amid the Southern light."

Newton Knight takes Hemmingway's African ivory star from the broken body of Charles Edward Franklin, and the spirit shoots it up to the top of the Christmas tree to the point of the tallest limb where it begins to glow. Then the Confederate ghost and the sparrow forever disappear from Fable Court out of the open side window.

DEAR READER, DECEMBER 28, 1960, OXFORD, MISSISSIPPI

Chapter 11

Looking back at Fable Court, none of us ever would have thought that things would have ended the way that they did. After Sheriff Delk heard the story, he decided to let sleeping dogs lie—or goddamn dead cowardly bastards sleep. He released Layne into the Farmer's care, providing they comply with Eleanor's last wish. Together, they accepted the burden of endurance and moved to my beloved Oxford where the many secrets of Eleanor's heart were revealed. I, along with Mordecai Malachi, cleaned up her mess. I guess it's fair to write—out of love.

When I contacted the Reverend Morty Rayborn over in Selma, Alabama, and his wife, Lucy, it struck me as queer that they didn't seem the least bit surprised to get my phone call. Said now they knew the reason that they had felt compelled to cut their vacation short, were still packed, and would drive back to Oxford overnight. The Rayborns agreed to preside over the Franklin's funeral at Saint Peter's Cemetery in Oxford, Mississippi, and accepted their gift of free land. Mary and Joe Farmer sat beside Layne, who looked sad in his own dimwitted way holding Julius Caesar who looked fine except for a broken front leg. Mordecai stood near the old shed wearing that goddamn gardener's suit like the eternal gravedigger he always was. After all, it had served him well.

After the Reverend Rayborn finished his sermon, everyone walked by a freshly dug grave and threw in a carnation, except for Mary who threw in a piece of wood. That December day was cold and blustery. Bone-chilling. But that's not what I remember most about it. No, it was the clay around the grave—red-orange, muddy. That stuck to my mind like good Scotch whiskey because I still can't figure out how it got so muddy, so quick. Maybe it was the drizzles of rain or from the melting of that first December's snow. I thought, "Why the holy hell did they dig it anyway? For show maybe?" Perhaps—since Eleanor Beatrice Godwin Franklin had requested in her will that she be put inside the longtime empty Franklin mausoleum on top of her dear, beloved Charles Edward amid their books beneath Claude Monet's Lavacourt: Sunshine and Snow after everyone left Saint Peter's Cemetery.

Chapter 12

T HE SUN IS SPINNING in a peacock blue sky over the Oxford highway where Reverend Morty and Lucy Rayborn are taking down the road sign that advertised the free land. Once it's down, they get into their car and ride back to a lilac Victorian house with black trim with a wrap-around porch that's nested in the tall Mississippi pines on the Franklin land. The house is a reasonable walking distance to Fable Court.

After the Rayborns do away with the road sign, they park themselves on the wrap-around front porch of their lilac house and begin rocking and talking. Although much of the snow has melted, about half an image of what used to be a whole snowman with a carrot sticking out from its melting face and a cigar steadied in one corner of its mouth remains in the front yard. Reverend Morty is reading a section of an *Oxford Eagle*. Lucy has a pair of scissors in one hand with the funny papers spread across her lap.

Reverend Morty tells his wife, "See. Lucy, you don't ever know what the good Lord has planned for His children that endure ... Look how we *endured* livin' in Selma, Alabama, all of them years!"

A salt-and-pepper Chihuahua climbs up the front steps and gives them a perky look before sitting down in front of the screen door. The Chihuahua wags his tail then barks, "Ruff!"

Lucy darts her eyes Reverend Morty's way but says nothing.

"Know what I mean, *Sugar?*"

Lucy looks across the Franklin land then up at the Mississippi sky and down at the *Oxford Eagle's* funny papers. She snickers a little and blows a fog of cold air onto her wedding band. She begins to polish it on an area of her shirt near her heart while looking at what's left of a melting snowman — the carrot.

While Reverend Morty waits for Lucy's answer, the Southern light begins to shine on her face, and for a moment, Morty's so blinded by the light and sparkle of two glowing diamonds that are dotting her ear lobes that he squints his eyes.

"Hell, Morty! It is commitment—pure commitment," she tells him, cracking her knuckles.

He flings her a sharp, agitated look, but doesn't speak.

IN DOWNTOWN OXFORD, Mordecai is standing at a window paying for a box of freshly baked tea biscuits and a loaf of pumpernickel bread. An elderly white-headed German woman with *Annabelle* embroidered in red on her white uniform can be seen taking two quarters from him while a somewhat retarded girl with *Violet* embroidered in green on a black uniform looks on. Before making change, Annabelle reaches into the base of her donut-shaped hair bun and secures the legs on a black hair pin. She hands Mordecai a shiny, silver dime. Triumphantly, he sets off on foot for Number 33 Fable Court with biscuits and bread in hand.

THE FARMERS, LAYNE, AND MORDECAI ARE LOOKING across a beautiful landscape patched with melted snow while black smoke rises from one of Fable Court's chimneys. Mary reaches into the melting snow and begins digging a hole and feeling around for something. Once she reaches the soil, she brings back a handful of dirt. She turns to Layne and says, "Layne, give me your hand."

Layne eyes her suspiciously with his left eye but gives her his hand.

In an optimistic, voice Mary says, "This is yours—all yours! Feel it! It is rich soil ready to plant and to reap a new harvest as soon as the snow melts and winter passes. Look, Layne, all this land is yours!"

He gives her a blank look.

She takes a deep breath in and says, "All you've got to do is thank the good Lord for it!"

Still, Layne shows no enthusiasm whatsoever. Instead, he looks to Joe for an out and unexpectedly shouts, *"Women!"*

Joe smiles, gets his signal, and offers, "Hey, Layne, you want to go with me to Rowan Oak to see William? We can walk though Bailey's Woods."

Layne claps his hands, and with a childish urgency, he says, "Let's go see Billy and his Jacks!"

Joe reaches for Mary's shoulder and draws her near to his face. He smiles, bends, and plants a kiss as light as the wind in the center of her forehead. "Babydoll, we'll be back in a little while, you hear?"

She nods, pleased at the growing friendship between the three.

Layne says, *"Babydoll?"*

The menfolk turn and walk off towards Bailey's Woods, leaving Mary standing alone until a blue jay flies up and lands on a solitary limb of what's left of an old Kieffer pear tree.

"What do *you* want?" she asked the solitary bird. "Where's your other half?"

At first, no noise comes but an echo of her own thin, wistful voice until, as if to make fun of her, the blue jay throws his head back and lets out a single, high derisive note. The limb breaks, and the blue jay flies off across Bailey's Woods towards William Faulkner's house, Rowan Oak. Mary reaches, picks up the broken limb, and twirls it between her fingers before turning and beginning her walk home to Fable Court.

ROWAN OAK—THE WRITING PORCH

Chapter 13

FOR MUCH OF THE AFTERNOON, Mordecai, Joe, and Layne have been sitting and talking with William Faulkner on his writing porch. Layne is holding one of the Christmas poodle puppies from Increase in his lap. The poodle puppy is wearing a red sweater with *JoJo* knitted in navy-blue across its back. Joe, who has Tippy, his Chihuahua, in his lap looks over and sees the silver slate Newton Knight left behind positioned upright on a table beside Faulkner's collection of soft drink bottle caps. A ray of sunlight is causing its sapphires to gleam and sparkle onto a copy of an *Oxford Eagle* dated January 1, 1961, that's neatly folded in half on the foot of

Faulkner's writing cot along with a stack of blank writing paper and sharpened pencils.

"Joe, my boy! I'm glad you and Mary decided to move to Oxford and look after Layne. If I can be of any help, well, you just let me know," William Faulkner says, nodding at Joe and turning to wink at Layne who waves at him and his Jack Russell Terriers.

Mordecai nods.

Layne smiles, pats the Christmas poodle puppy, and then considers his thoughts for a minute before reaching into his shirt pocket and pulling out a $20 gold certificate, handing it to Faulkner. He asks him, "Scotch?!"

"Good God, man! Where did you get this?!" Faulkner asks.

"Newton Knight gave it to me," Layne answers proudly, left eye gleaming like the sun.

"That figures," Faulkner remarks before reading from the bill. *Twenty-dollars in gold coin ... 1863.* Hell, Layne! You are rich now, aren't you?!"

Layne says, "No words, no words! Hush,"

Faulkner shakes his head and sighs. He asks Joe, "Joe, my boy, now that you have been given the gift of time, tell me, have you given much thought to writing? What are your thoughts worth to you?"

Layne speaks up, "A penny!"

Everyone laughs.

Joe looks at the walls of Faulkner's writing porch and sees various pieces of paper hung up with the days of the week printed across their tops. On one piece of paper, he reads to himself, *Belladonna, neighbor, the boy, truth, butcher knife, pear tree, and cowardly bastard*. He sees A *Fable* penciled in graphite and plaster on the wall. There is one volume of something by William Shakespeare with a worn spine making the title unreadable. He reaches for a blank piece of paper at the foot of the cot, takes a sharpened pencil from inside of the glass jar that once held Eleanor Franklin's "mint-flavored" snuff, and begins scribbling on the blank page. He motions for Layne to hand it to Faulkner while saying, "You better believe I have!" He sets his eyes on an empty wrought-iron bird cage in the far corner of the porch with an engraved bronze nameplate that reads *Cordelia* sitting next to a framed and wrinkled crayon portrait of William Faulkner signed *Layne* before he asks him, "Billy, will you help me?"

Mordecai raises his eyebrows.

Layne continues patting JoJo with one hand while handing Faulkner Joe's piece of paper with the other. Faulkner reads what Joe has written to himself and gives an approving nod before handing the piece of paper back to Layne. He gives them a right eye wink along with a tight smile before asking, "Layne, can you read what's written on this piece of paper?"

Layne moves forward and reads aloud four words, "Southern Light, Oxford, Mississippi."

Everyone smiles including Mordecai, when with lifted eyebrows William Faulkner takes the pencil from Joe, breaks it, and says not a word more.

THE END

Teaching Recommendation for *Southern Light, Oxford, Mississippi*

Southern Light, Oxford, Mississippi is a novel which best fits into the Southern Gothic genre and should be taught as such. The title itself suggests the Southern mystique which infuses the novel, the unexplainable and supernatural impact of place and spirit which controls people and events of the novel. The novel might best be used in a college American Literature curriculum at the junior-or-senior-level. Too, it could be very effective in a graduate-level seminar.

The instructor/facilitator of the book should introduce the novel through lecture with accompanying handouts to reinforce the discussion/overview of the basic elements of the Southern Gothic genre:

> *Setting*: foreboding atmosphere including location, structures, and mood
> *Characters*: eccentric, often grotesque, and unstable eliciting both repulsion and compassion
> *Plots*: disturbing events, often supernatural and suddenly bizarre
> *Themes*: disturbed psyches and violent events
> *Mood/Tone*: depression, oppression, and isolation juxtaposed against dark humor

Southern Light, Oxford, Mississippi is rich in Gothic elements being set in Oxford, Mississippi, in the most *Southern* of the South—near the campus of the University of Mississippi, a locale steeped in 1) tradition from eccentricities of intellectuals, 2) the lore of the Civil War, 3) a privileged landed gentry, 4) a history of racial intolerance, and 5) superstition.

There is in the novel an uneasy intrigue which moves the story from its eccentric beginning to its truly Gothic conclusion. The broad setting—the houses with shaded lanes of ancient moss-draped trees on the outskirts of the Ole Miss, the homes of Eleanor, Charles Edward, and Layne Franklin and neighboring William Faulkner—provides for the eccentric and threatening elements of the novel.

In using the novel in a college setting, an instructor would have many areas to explore through the lecture/note-taking format or a seminar approach with students writing on recurrent themes within the book. Perhaps the best approach to teaching the novel is employment of both ways: 1) lecture introduction by the instructor, 2) instructor identification of themes and allowance for student discovery, 3) assignment of student-generated formal papers of a minimum of five-pages analyzing a specific thread/theme throughout the novel.

Below are examples of broad subjects/elements which students may explore in formulating their essays:

1. Elements of the *Southern Light, Oxford, Mississippi* placing it in the Gothic genre

2. Symbolism in the novel (Light, snow, cardinal, *King Lear*, red-orange clay, dark spectacles, sparrow, December eye-bleeding, poetry, writing, love-hate.)
3. Psychological studies of a major character (Eleanor, Faulkner, Layne, Mordecai)
4. Identification of words peculiar to the sixties' South (parlor, dark spectacles, hokey, Lord ah mercy, Lord in heaven, lick-a-dee split, picture show, land sakes alive, take the cake)
5. Comparison of *Southern Light, Oxford, Mississippi* to a Faulkner, O'Connor, or Lee work
6. The Gothic conceptualization of a small Southern town
7. *Southern Light, Oxford, Mississippi* as an exposure of unacceptable social conditions in the Deep South
8. Historical representation of the South in "Southern Light, Oxford, Mississippi"

Students would present their papers in seminar fashion, allowing for a full discussion and understanding of the novel.

FORTHCOMING BY THE AUTHOR

MY NEIGHBORS, GOODLIFE, MISSISSIPPI

BATTLE FOR LOVE   A NOVEL

Milton Keynes UK
Ingram Content Group UK Ltd.
UKHW022325141123
432592UK00004B/73